FORCED TO SPY

Berlin: 1941

Sandy Santora and Judy Green

ISBN 13: 9781796724899

FORCED TO SPY
Berlin, Early 1941

PROLOGUE

Born in 1889.

Baptized a Catholic.

Father was a low-level customs official who had been born out of wedlock.

Received low grades in school.

Failed the entrance exam at the Academy of Arts.

Took menial jobs to earn a living.

Failed to join his country's military.

Spent months in prison.

His name was Adolf Hitler, and he came into power as Chancellor of Germany in 1933.

This is not a story about Adolf Hitler.

We want the context of our story to bring you into this time period, and set the stage for our spy novel of suspense. Bring your thoughts back to this era of the turbulence-taking place in Germany at that time.

It was a time of political chaos, of massive unemployment, millions were near starvation and hysteria was gripping the nation.

It was ripe for a savior who could unite the masses. Yes, this same man would wreak havoc on the rest of the world.

His oratory was hypnotic and millions mesmerized by his powerful speeches. Thousands stood for hours as excitement and fever filled the arena. However, behind these fiery bursts of Nationalism, stood the world's **demon of darkness**.

CHAPTER ONE

Always plotting to destroy his perceived enemies, he was secretly building all types of warfare.

In pursuit of his goal he left no stone unturned. Always scheming with thoughts of treachery, he called in one of his men, "I hear there's a man experimenting with rockets."

"Yes, I've been told there is."

"Who is he?"

"His name is Werhner von Braun and he's an Aerospace Engineer. My people tell me he's an expert in rocketry."

"Um, rockets. Can we arm them with explosives? If we can, it would be a way to eliminate those who stand against us. Germany's enemies."

Later, Hitler's question was answered.

"Yes, these can be armed with tons of explosives."

A jubilant Chancellor banged his fists on the desk, "We will build these rockets.

"We will give the money to von Braun to build these glorious weapons."

He funded the rocketry development with huge sums of revenue to support his mission.

Years passed as von Braun struggled with his rocketry program. By the end of 1940, Hitler became impatient and frustrated and cut their funds dramatically. He gave von Braun one last chance – one more year to prove that the rockets could be operational.

The deadline loomed large over von Braun as he thought to himself, "I need help and I need it now!"

Through his connections, he heard of a theoretical physicist who was actually working on the very component with which he was having difficulty.

His name was Emil Brandt. He lived and worked in Berlin and maybe he would be the answer.

Von Braun contacted a liaison and requested an urgent meeting with Emil Brandt.

A STAR IS BORN.

Emil Brandt was from a middle class German family. He was born in 1916 to Margaret and Herlich Brandt. He was the youngest of four brothers who were fighting for Germany during World War 1. Even at a young age, he took great pride in his brothers who were sacrificing their lives for the love of their country. Brandt's parents noticed that their youngest boy possessed an extraordinary mind and knew they must further his education. Even with their modest income, they were able to send their gifted son to the acclaimed Friedrich-Wilhelm's University.

He graduated with a high honors as a theoretical physicist at the impressive age of twenty, and went on to join a group of notable scientists where his contribution was quickly apparent.

Emil Brandt was brilliant, handsome, physically strong and Hitler's version of the true Aryan. He was six feet tall and had adapted the aristocratic carriage that he so admired, along with an attitude of superiority. Penetrating green eyes, chiseled features and a sultry mouth were a magnet for women. He, in return, loved their attention.

Having been a quiet student, Emil Brandt was now a confident leader in his field. Other scientists were in awe of his remarkable theories. Soon he would be working on the most complex and important achievement of his life.

He was thrilled to be a part of Germany's future, his beloved Germany.

He was working on the exact theory of rocketry that was eluding von Braun. He could be the key to unlocking the problem. The meeting was set up for the two men to meet and join forces.

Brandt, stationed in Berlin, now worked in concert with von Braun who was in Peenemunde, on the Baltic Sea, where the rockets were being tested. Brandt could supply the scientific knowledge that would open the door to the final and terrifying conclusion.

England, now fully in the grip of war, and America on the verge of war, watched with total awareness of this growing threat from their alliance.

This must be stopped at all costs. As this collaboration formed, another began on the other side of the world.

BRITISH AND AMERICANS
JOIN FORCES

CHAPTER TWO

As Hitler's wartime conquests began to explode, British agents from MI6 became aware of Germany's developments in rocketry, continuing their country's further domination.

A British double agent in Berlin, working undercover in Emil Brandt's lab, became aware of the union of these two exceptional minds. He realized this partnership could pose a deadly threat to England.

Since von Braun was working in Peenemunde, he was unreachable. Therefore, Emil Brandt, working in Berlin, would be their objective.

Target: Emil Brandt

England was fearful that the Germans were becoming increasing cognizant of their operatives from MI6. They were afraid that both their men and women were in jeopardy of being exposed.

Therefore, a new coalition of British and American agents were formed. Working together, an intricate plan was woven.

This new team needed to be formed with America's top secret agent Joe Matthews at the helm. He was to lead a prominent and highly dangerous role in the upcoming engagement.

How to infiltrate this liaison between von Braun and Brandt was the main topic of consideration. Many options were considered and rejected.

One of the options brought to their attention came to them through a German couple now working for the British. Their insider information gave them knowledge of Brandt's breakup of a love affair with a German woman named Marta Brauer.

Therefore, the link to Brandt should be a woman. Marta Brauer would now be the gateway to bringing an American woman into Brandt's life. It was decided that it had to be an American woman of high intellect and striking looks who would be the key to seducing Brandt.

She had to be highly educated in mathematics and science. Only then would she be in a position to decipher his hypothesis. They would discover later that their choice would also possess an exceptional memory.

Our plot will commence with Marta Brauer, German citizen.

Christine Spencer, the chosen American.

MARTA'S COMMITMENT

CHAPTER THREE

Marta Brauer, Berlin, early 1941. Berlin was cold. A deadly quiet hung over the streets with pedestrians walking quickly to their destination.

Marta felt eyes peering out at her through shuttered windows. Why this fear? She was, after all, an attractive young woman from a good Christian family. However, Marta had a secret. A dangerous secret that could ultimately destroy her.

As she accelerated her walk with heels, resounding through the cobblestone streets, she was afraid that the next sound she would hear would be the Gestapo. Her thoughts over the last month were vivid and unrelenting. Never would she forget the night of the commitment she made when first approached......

..."Marta, Marta, can't you hear the doorbell ringing? Get the door. You know I cannot move easily from this chair" The paternal voice was as abrupt and cold as Berlin. "I'm sorry father; I was listening to the radio".

When she opened the door, two men in dark nondescript suits stood in the doorway as one said to her in German, "Marta Brauer? Are you Marta Brauer?

The man asking her was immediately struck by the face staring at him as soon as she opened the door. Her hair shimmered in the low lighting, but it was clearly filled with golden strands. She was not a true beauty, but certainly one that would be called attractive. Her features were just a bit pronounced leaving her eyes of dark blue her best feature. Dressed in a loose fitting garment it was difficult to see the lines of her curvaceous body.

Her automatic sense of legitimate terror answered with, "Yes, I'm Marta Brauer. What do you want?"

"We must speak with you," as they firmly moved their way into the small yet tidy room, "and it's private". Her legs were beginning to tremble and her words shaky and fearful, "Please show me some identification". A wallet was drawn from one of the men and when she saw the card, her quickened heartbeat settled down.

This was not the Gestapo, but it set off a new set of alarms. Was this really happening? Was she prepared to embrace the new life she had been waiting for?

Marta bowed her head slightly and motioned the men to sit on the couch. She then went to the kitchen where her father sat and said, "Father, isn't Herr Brennen alone tonight? He asks me all the time for you to come by. Please, pay him a visit now and make him happy."

"Who are those men, Marta?"

"They work with me. We need to go over some papers I typed. You know how critical any errors can be. Please, they won't be able to tell me what they need me to revise while you're here".

Herr Brauer didn't want to know. He struggled to stand up from his chair and moved to the door, not turning towards the men and abruptly closed it behind him.

Once he had left, one of the men, whose identification revealed that he was British agent named Harold Porter leaned toward Marta and spoke intently, "We understand you were having a relationship with a man called Emil Brandt and that this man was introduced to you by a couple named Schmidt a few months ago".

As soon as Porter mentioned the name Emil Brandt, Marta felt her heart quicken and body quietly shake. He was the man she was in love with. He was the man who rejected her after she had confessed her true feelings.

"Brandt is the reason we need to see you, and in return for your help we are prepared to promise you a life outside Germany, something we know you want".

She knew Emil was important but never could she imagine just how essential he must be to warrant such a promise.

"We are also well aware of how fond you are of the Schmidts as they are of you.

"Here is letter from Herr Schmidt he wants you to read." As Marta took the letter from its envelope, her thoughts drifted back to the memory of how they had enhanced her life. ....

..... As a government employee, she was required to attend all functions and receptions. At a small gathering one evening at a celebration for the Third Reich, she was just standing in a corner, quite alone as usual. She was startled to recognize one of the NAZI Officers. She remembered seeing him laughing as he and his fellow NAZI's dragged a terrified family through the street into a waiting vehicle. This was just one of the incidents she had witnessed as her illusions vanished and were replaced by fear.

For the moment, her fears abated when she was approached by a lovely couple with an offering of a small glass of sherry. She admired the handsome couple clearly old enough to be her parents and found herself drawn to their warmth. The evening turned out to be easy and comfortable. Talking to this couple for nearly two hours, she felt a strong desire to see them again.

Frau Schmidt said,

"We would like you to meet an eligible single gentlemen whom I'm sure would find you very attractive."

Marta did not to know that she was specifically chosen to become the link to Emil Brandt.

Who were the Schmidts?

They both came from wealthy families and enjoyed a privileged lifestyle in Germany, a lifestyle allowing them the invitations to receptions and parties where they overheard the outpouring of stories where brutal tactics were becoming commonplace. Their disillusionment led to the fear of Hitler's new policies.

Feeling they must share this information with the British, they travelled to London to meet with an old friend who was high positioned in the War Department. He thanked them and said that he would share what they told him with his colleagues and certainly would get back to them.

Of course, the War Department was excited to hear about firsthand information coming from the German hierarchy. After much debate, they came to a unanimous decision to ask them to become informants for the British government.

The Schmidts agreed with alacrity.

The British would determine exactly what role they could play. They followed orders and pretended to comply with the very men they despised. Keeping a social connection was their doorway to information.

Emil Brandt was their objective. They were instructed to find and encourage a woman whom they could introduce to Emil Brandt. They needed someone who could obtain even minimal information about his comings and goings.

This could prove important for any future plans.......

.....As Marta continued reading the letter from Herr Schmidt, the British agent said, "Besides the letter they have told us the countless times how you quietly and often indirectly spoke of your wish to leave Germany. I believe your trust in the Schmidts made it possible to be honest, otherwise you would never have been so candid had you not truly trusted them to protect your wishes."

Now allowing her to continue reading, they quietly waited, with apprehension, for her to finish the words written in the handwriting she recognized.

As she was reading, the other agent was trying to understand if and why she would betray her country since her life seemed to suggest a world sufficient with the trappings of the establishment she now lived in. On some level, she was an ideal spokesperson for the Reich. Attractive, well educated, however, deeply distressed about the new regime.

Marta had been raised in a home where her parents rigidly followed the patterns of their own upbringing exhibiting insensitive feelings with only a minimal need to converse. They mindlessly acquiesced to the dictates of the time in which they resided.

Marta was born less than a year after World War 1 and her family barely existed in a country burdened with the uncertainty of necessities and political chaos. Their stagnant faces transferred to the child to whom they felt resentment.

Marta was not a wanted addition and her essentials often deprived them of the little they had. Both parents never felt the bond of closeness with their pretty offspring and Marta grew up distant, without experiencing intimacy and approval.

Even with her unsatisfied upbringing Marta was such a good student that when she reached the age of twenty her advancement in the financial section of the local government office gave her a small sense of accomplishment. Enough to permit her access to celebrations where she would meet people and discover just how much she found their views to give her great cause for trepidation.

The next time she saw the Schmidts it was at their invitation to a reception. The three were sharing cocktails toward the rear of the room when Frau Schmidt said, "Oh Marta over there is Emil; he is the man I was telling you about. He has been at several of these receptions. He is the man I would like to introduce to you. Why doesn't Herr Schmidt make the introduction. Claus, go and ask him to join us. He is standing alone and now would be a good time. Is that okay with you Marta?" After a quick glance, she nodded yes. Herr Schmidt caught the eye of Brandt as he was walking in their direction.

After they all chatted for a while and assured that Brandt was not going to run off too quickly, the Schmidts made their excuses and departed.

Standing alone with Emil, Marta felt intrigued by the attention he was paying her. "My god he's so handsome and confident," she told herself. She almost could not believe that he didn't find an excuse to vanish. He spent the next couple of hours actually enjoying her company. She held her breath at one point hoping and praying he would ask to see her again. When the words finally came from him as the evening ended, she just wanted to grab hold of the moment and bring it to her bed later when she could dream.

Her dream did not last long. Two months later after seeing Emil on a somewhat regular basis, she muttered the words 'I love you' that would end his infatuation for her. Emil was not interested in anyone who loved him. He was not interested in anyone who showed him any honest emotion. Emil found himself, as usual with women, finding a list of faults that added up to their removal from his life.

Therefore, the agents did not need to threaten Marta. She would acquiesce to whatever they wanted her to do. She would leave the country that offered her nothing but fear and despair.

Soon she would be informed of the role she was to play.

She would get back at Emil for hurting her.

JULES WHITE AND ARTHUR LEMBECK

CHAPTER FOUR

Jules White, a senior American agent, stared out the window as the airplane began its descent to the ground. The New York skyline engulfed the air below as he thought about the weight of his work ahead.

Jules was an ideal choice for recruiting candidates; for those who might need to be approached through persuasion or coercion.

He thoroughly reviewed his documents as the limousine drove him to his suite at the Drake Hotel. He thought to himself, "I see that the proposed candidate is coming through Arthur." He said to himself, "That's good, Arthur is a great researcher." Arthur Lembeck was put into his current position because in his earlier and non-governmental career he had years of employment in privately owned companies as the man in charge of personnel and then security. This experience base today gave him an instant advantage for vetting any candidate deemed important enough to consider. He had already displayed his impeccable judgment when investigating the need for a very specific and detailed assessment of a prospective candidate.

Finally, in his room waiting for Arthur, Jules paced back and forth and tried to contain his excitement, "After all Arthur would never be so optimistic if it wasn't a serious lead. But what if.....I have to stop this nagging worry."

Jules picked up the ringing telephone to receive word from downstairs that Arthur was on his way up. Minutes later Arthur entered the suite wearing his usual dark blue suit, crisp white shirt that was topped off with a plain medium blue tie. It seemed like his uniform and Jules thought he must have had a closet full of dark blue suits and crisp white shirts. The medium blue ties were probably lined up in a row alongside the black shoes he always wore. His outfit reflected Arthur's impression of himself and he would soon impress Jules.

"Nice to see you again, Arthur."

Cursory greetings were exchanged since they both eagerly wanted to start the meeting.

Jules started,

"First, tell me exactly how you decided that this is your choice."

"My task was difficult."

Jules interrupts,

"What was your difficulty, Arthur?"

"Let me explain. First of all very few universities and colleges are open to women and those majoring in mathematics are few and far between.

"My staff approached deans and professors using the guise of seeking a candidate for a very important government position."

"Okay, Arthur, that sounds like a good beginning. How did this eventually bring us to your preference?"

"Only one university fit our criteria."

"In what way?"

"Well, our prospective candidate, Christine Spencer, is academically and physically perfect for the role. An added bonus is that she comes from a German speaking family and she is fluent in the Germanic language."

"Is she really good looking enough to attract Brandt?"

Arthur, then with a flourish, tossed the picture of Christine onto the table.

Jules just stared in disbelief.

"Well Arthur, you outdid yourself."

Jules continued,

"Tell me slowly without missing the tiniest detail everything you know about her."

"She's a graduate student at Cornell University where she is working toward her doctorate in science and a secondary emphasis in Applied Mathematics. Her references from every teacher are exceptional. Don't worry, I told them she was being considered for a high ranking position in the State Department after she graduates.

"She appears to have a real passion for problem solving and asks questions that demonstrate she has a very unique and abstract way to interpret problems."

Jules interrupted, "Her aptitude for numbers is obviously essential, but what about her memory? She needs to translate and interpret an enormous amount of data."

Arthur immediately jumped in with, "Her memory is amazing.

"As a matter of fact at one of the meetings with her mathematics professor, he blurted out that she has shown an extraordinary ability for complex thinking and her memory is phenomenal."

He prodded Arthur to continue his reporting......

"Her given name is Christine Anne Spencer. She was born on June, 7, 1919 in Chicago to Robert and Elizabeth Spencer. Standard upbringing in an affluent suburb.

"Pretty rigid childhood as far as I can tell.

"At an early age, five maybe six, her intelligence was obvious. Reading years ahead of others, it was the math that was almost eerie to her teachers.

"She began to blossom even more fully when she was separated from her parents. Whatever the reason, she became very serious about advancing her skills, certainly in math and science, and that's what we're most interested in.

"Her beauty aroused jealousy among her female contemporaries and she never formed any real friendships.

"Although she dated, there were no serious relationships until college."

"Ok, tell me Arthur."

"It was her third year at Cornell. She was attracted to a student she met in her Economics class. Handsome and popular, he was sought after by the female student body. When he saw Christine for the first time, he knew he had to have her. He bragged to his friends, "she's going to be mine." Although she did date him, she made it very difficult, often either not available or cancelling their date.

"After finally allowing herself to be seduced by him she found out he was sleeping with other ladies. She threw him aside to his utter devastation and her disillusionment.

She refused to see him again".

Interrupting Arthur, "How could you possibly know that about this guy?"

"It was the talk of the school."

"Ok, now continue. What about her home life?"

"A close relationship with her mother but a cold unyielding father who gave her very little attention and approval."

"What was the makeup of the family?"

"Mother, father and grandparents.

"The grandparents emigrated from Germany and spoke very little English. That is why Christine became fluent in German."

"Now that's a coup."

BERLIN BOMBED

CHAPTER FIVE

Jules and Arthur continued their discussion well through the night.

While they conferred about Christine on one continent, across another continent a team of German scientists feverishly worked to complete the next stage of von Braun's deadline.

It was the first month in 1941 and 10 months before the United States would enter the war. Germany now occupied vast stretches of Europe with its' capture of major countries like Poland, France, Norway, Belgium, Denmark, Holland, leaving other countries to wait helplessly for their grasp.

Now Hitler set his sights on England and might have succeeded in the Battle of Britain if it weren't for the incredible bravery of the Royal Air Force (RAF). In retaliation for the bombing of England the RAF ferociously bombed Berlin.

Berlin was still cold and damp in January. The bombing raids from England had affected Berlin, but the German population never doubted a victorious outcome.

The bombing, fortunately for the German people, did not do great damage tonight.

Von Braun's team in Peenemunde were relieved that a particular building in Berlin, and its deep foundation, was saved.

This nondescript structure on 4 Durchgehen Street housed an important handpicked group of scientists headed by Emil Brandt.

In order to pass through the front door an SS guard would check their identification. A strict policy enacted every time no matter how many times they recognized the individual.

A second locked door opened revealing a staircase leading down to the bunker beneath the earth. There the exclusive assemblage of German scientists would spend their days and oftentimes nights.

Emil Brandt's outward confidence and demeanor only enhanced his masculine and stunning appearance that actually caused concern among some. One could never be quite sure of what lies behind the eyes, mouth and voice.

He sits among his fellow colleagues and smiles to himself. He is very pleased, very pleased indeed. He is the leader of the group. He is the one, the one with the original idea and it is ingenious. He knows that when solved, he will please von Braun beyond anything he could have imagined.

Had he known of the plot that was forming against him, his confidence would have been thoroughly shaken.

JOE MATTHEWS,
WASHINGTON, DC

CHAPTER SIX

After Joe Matthews met with the representatives from England and the United States, he returned to his apartment in Washington, D.C. where he was required to live, as he was on constant call.

He cautiously closed the door and proceeded to check his surroundings in the habitual way he did every time. As soon as he finished checking, he allowed himself a well-needed respite.

His reclining position on the bed did not last long. He sprang up and reached for the small bottle on his dresser that housed the medicine he needed to relieve the pain in his stomach he was now experiencing. He was diagnosed with an ulcer that could have led to the end of his career in the field. He would keep the diagnosis a secret and hoped that the doctor gave him enough pills to get him through the assignment.

After swallowing the pill, it wasn't long before he found the relief he depended on and he could allow his mind to find its way to each piece of the plan with near disbelief at the intricacies involved. However, he and only he could manage to bring them all together. His dogged controlled thinking and ability to execute them made him the ideal choice; a choice they would never have been willing to make had his health ever been an issue.

Joe was convinced he could keep his illness at bay long enough to complete the work that was expected of him. There was no other alternative for a man who felt his country was threatened.

Joe was enhanced in his work by his warm and personable appearance. He was not truly handsome but even at 5' 10" his demeanor was inviting. His dark brown eyes could see right through you. Even just a glance could throw you off guard. His smile was engaging and could charm friend as well as enemy. Due to his immense amount of physical training his body was taut and perfectly toned.

As soon as World War 1 ended he had accelerated his studies and received an education that would offer his government a very accomplished asset who could work clandestinely.

Now in the room he allowed the pills to work their magic. Just as he finally drifted off, he said a small prayer to remain healthy enough to accomplish his task.

He was awakened by the returning pain.

Joe was feeling more anxiety since the pains he needed to relieve with medication seem to be coming more often. He kept ordering and drinking milk as his doctor advised and thought to himself how he needed to calm his thoughts. Being so anxious only added to the illness.

Waiting to hear from him, with the final chosen candidate, only added to his anxiety.

He threw on his coat and left the room to walk outside.

The streets of D.C. seem to advertise their familiar and spotless exterior that surrounded the unblemished and intact buildings. It contrasted to how some unfortunate cities in Europe were caught in a trap of destruction.

He needed, however, to clear his mind and focus on the feats to be administered and performed in the coming months.

The cool air seem to bring his thoughts into sharp focus that centered on his mission: Emil Brandt.

Since the most significant part of the operation would revolve around Jules' candidate, he could permit his thoughts to wander back to a time of his one love.....

.....It was August 15, 1918 when the government arranged for Joe to work as an engineer in a small company in New York. This company had been linked to the illegal sale of technical data being secretly transmitted outside the United States. Joe was there to gather information.

Even in peacetime, it was a great responsibility for one so young.

Joe's cover as an engineer was gratifying but not his only source of pleasure. He also enjoyed the company of women and women certainly enjoyed his company as well.

However, none would remain in his heart until he was just past twenty-three.

Even when on assignment Joe would socialize with one woman or another. Tonight it was going to be Joanna, until her phone call came and she asked for a rain check. She was sick and needed to stay in bed with a fever that wouldn't break.

Still wanting to see the movie, he made his way to the theater. After taking his seat, he glanced to his right where two women sat. One older at his far right and one nearly touching his right arm.

He tried not to look at her in the darkness that was lit slightly from the projected images on the screen, but her delicate profile forced his eyes to turn to her.

Finally, the movie ended and lights went on. Now he could see if his imagination was playing tricks. It was not. Her face met his almost instantaneously and a spark moved between them. They both seemed to experience a familiarity hardly found among strangers, but it was there. His eyes commanded the gaze to remain until the older woman summoned her.

With a pronounced accent,

"Lee, come on, we have to get back to the hotel. What are you doing?"

Joe actually pulled out his card and scribbled on the back the name and address of a restaurant, slipped it into her hand, leaned toward her and as he did he whispered, "I know this sounds crazy, but I'll be at this restaurant tomorrow night and I'll wait for you all night. Please come". Joe looked as Lee slipped the card into her pocket with a hint of a smile and she purposely did not nod since it might be seen by her mother.

At that same time, her mother tugged at Lee's arm and continued, "Let's go". As they moved away she said, "I cannot believe you would even look at a complete stranger, let alone listen to him. What did he say to you?"

"I don't know, something about how he thought I was pretty. You know I can take care of myself."

"Oh no you can't."

All the way back to the hotel Lee was trying to unravel the feeling she was experiencing since it never happened to her before.

There was someone waiting for her back home, someone who never made her feel this way. All she could think about was the whispered voice of the stranger while at the same time worrying her mother sensed something. Her mother would surely have done anything to prevent any contact between them. After all, the man back home, Robert, was her mother's choice for Lee.

In her mother's presence, Lee tried to act as though nothing had changed. However, there was no hiding to herself that a new sensation had found its way through her. She felt flushed as she turned away from her mother's eyes trying to probe and dominate her.

She slipped her hand back into her coat pocket where the card rested and her fingers could move gently around the edges. She couldn't wait to be alone to think about finding a way to meet him tomorrow. She would have to be inventive with her excuse and so she would rehearse beforehand and try to predict any problems.

This was not the first time she had to maneuver the truth. It had become second nature to her since she was all too familiar with the way her mother parented. Lee's father played a minor role in her upbringing, leaving the decisions to her mother. Her strict obedience was the cornerstone of the household and she adhered to its boundaries with exemplary behavior. Walking through the steps of constant approval left her nearly exhausted on a daily basis, but she did what she was told.

Even today in her early twenties, she attended a college close to home. It was a school where she could live at home and commute each day. Since her mother manipulated her choices in gentlemen callers, it was no surprise that there would be an engagement between Lee and Robert. Robert was a reasonably attractive young man whose future was solidified by the fact that his father owned the store where he would be working. Mother was encouraged by her daughter's secure future.

Lee liked Robert, she liked him a lot. She was, however, not feeling the way a stranger in a movie theater had made her feel just hours ago, not even close.

Fortunately, according to her mother, there would be plenty of time for marriage since mother wanted Lee to complete her education. It was getting close, and her mother felt the treat of a lovely week in New York with her daughter would be the perfect gift for Lee's excellent grades the past semesters.

The meeting at the movie happened on the third day of their trip, and Lee was preparing to find a way to meet her stranger.

As the evening approached, a surprise presented itself without any devious effort. Her mother was experiencing one of her migraine headaches and needed to take the medicine prescribed for use on rare occasions. Fortunate for Lee her mother did not forget the pills, those lovely pills that would surely put her mother into a sound sleep.

Lee waited impatiently until her mother had drifted off through the night. She made sure the lights were off, and the drapes drawn, before she closed the door behind her and headed outside the hotel and to one of the taxis parked in front. It moved too slowly, and yet not slow enough for her to float in a sea of fantasizing what it would be like to see him.

Joe too was fantasizing and then started to feel insecure about her being able, and even wanting to see him. He stood in front of Rums' Restaurant after checking inside for her and then paced back and forth until about 7:30pm when the lady appeared in a taxi. Swallowing his worry with a smile and extending his hand to help her, he now stood face to face with a woman who seemed to surpass anything he had been imagining.

After what seemed like a single moment in time, their words seem to flow seamlessly. It was as if these two people had known each other for years. Her enchanting face came to life with each sentence and his eyes relished their response. They were so engrossed that they were still standing outside deep in conversation a half hour later. A quick laugh of recognition that the restaurant was there waiting for their entry seemed to be a temporary intrusion into their private space.

His heart stopped a moment when she told him her visit would be ending in three days. The time they would be able to squeeze out would be limited and precious. They began to make plans.

It would seem strange to most anyone to be making plans, but not to these two people who seem to fit together effortlessly. It was such a change for Joe to feel as though all the women he knew simply never existed. He wanted to ask her to run away with him, now, but his rational side, his commitment to his government brought him back to reality. He would find a way to get the next few day off and then talk about their future.

They spent the last hour in planning how and when they would meet the next day. A block before he left her in front of her hotel they stopped walking, faced each other, moved close and held tight until they felt their long awaited moment for the kiss. They didn't want to stop kissing, holding, touching, but they would have to separate tonight and wait until tomorrow, and tomorrow she would not even try to resist the inevitable.

The next day all of Lee's energy was spent in providing a time away from her mother. The only excuse her mother would allow would be Lee attending a lecture being held at a school many blocks away. Her mother supported all things academic. Lee went on and on about the a subject her mother had no interest in but would serve Lee well for the hours she would be away.

Lee headed for the coffee shop that Joe had suggested they meet. They were going to spend the day taking in some of New York's highlights, but the moment they saw each other the plan quickly changed and they headed for a place to be alone, an address where Joe lived.

Joe unlocked his door and they fell into each other's arms.

The ticking moments they were able to spend were so intimate that the words, 'I love you' insisted they be spoken. Their intensity revealed an awareness of what this must be like to feel united with another. It would go on for hours and leave them only wanting more. They would find a way to see each other tomorrow.

During the short times between lovemaking, they talked about the future. They knew they would be together soon. Even though Joe knew she would have to leave, he would see her soon, go to where she lived and of course write her every day. His heart was hers. When she finally had to go, she felt positive about her new future and it sustained her when they separated.

It would be only two days after Lee left that the call came through to Joe. An important overseas assignment would take precedence over his personal life. He dare not call since he feared her mother might answer the phone, and so he sent her a letter. This letter to Lee Bachman explained that he could not be in touch until he returned to the States, but he would write often. He loved her dearly. He kept his fingers crossed that Lee would be there when he returned.

Her mother, in the meantime, discovered the letter from Joe before Lee could see it. She opened and read the words that explained an order for him to go abroad, but would contact her as soon as he could. Lee's mother, after the shock of knowing her daughter had deceived her in New York with this man, instantly destroyed the letter that would never reach the eyes of her daughter. After that first letter, she was always alert for the mail, her mother made sure that Lee would never see another word from this man.

Lee could not believe that she had not heard from Joe. Why hadn't he called her? Had she deceived herself into believing that he really loved her?

She was devastated. Unsuspecting of her mother's deviousness, she was heart-broken and felt rejected.

Gradually her love turned to bitterness and within the next couple of months, she would marry Robert.

Months later after Joe returned he could not reach the woman he loved. The response from her mother on the phone when he called her house, simply said she had married and moved away.

He nearly collapsed with the news of her marriage but could do nothing. He just had to feel the pain of losing the love of his life.

Now, in 1941 ....

.........The thought of Lee and never knowing what happened to her found its way into Joe's mind as it did so often. He had to force himself back to the current day and the reality of his mission.

FORCED PARTICIPATION

CHAPTER SEVEN

"Miss Spencer," Doctor Larson called out softly, so as not to disturb the class. No one stirred. Again, "Miss Spencer", this time a little louder.

The heads, bent over their microscopes did not seem to even hear him. With one exception. A blond head lifted and turned towards the doctor's voice. As always, Doctor Larson gave a very tiny gasp as the radiant face of Christine Spencer smiled at him. Dressed in a long white starched lab coat, her hair tied neatly in a bun at the back of her head, he was captivated by her beauty.

She stood and said questioningly, "You called me, Doctor?"

"Yes, Miss Spencer, the Dean has requested your presence in his office."

Christine's smile faded as she gave a startled look at the professor.

"The Dean wants me?"

"Yes, Miss Spencer, right now."

Christine removed her lab coat, folded it neatly and put it on her chair.

"Do you know why?"

"No, I'm not privy to that information. Just go no now, please."

Walking out the door Christine began to get an anxious feeling in her stomach. A few steps into the hall and she felt her legs dragging. The walk to the Dean's office would take about ten minutes.

She thought, "Did I do something wrong? It cannot be my work. Could it be the subject of my thesis? Well, I'll soon find out."

Dean Harding was sitting at his desk with another man whom he then introduced to Christine as Jules White. "Mr. White is a representative of the U.S. government and would like to meet with you privately."

The Dean believed that it involved a position for Christine in the State Department. Jules had led him to believe that she was being courted.

The Dean then continued, "Mr. White, you can both use my private study. I will be right next door if you have any questions."

As they walked to the study a shiver went down her spine as she thought, "What is this? Does it have to do with my coming from a German family? Would it inhibit my future?"

Now in the study, Jules motioned for her to sit. He thought, "even without makeup her picture doesn't do her justice." He had decided to take a non-threatening approach, for now.

Noticing her nervous demeanor, he spoke in a measured tone.

"Christine, may I call you Christine?"

"Of course."

"I've been hearing great things about you and your commendable academic abilities."

Christine's face that had turned a slight shade of red relaxed and her breathing slowed as she smiled.

"Thank you."

"That's the reason I'm here today to speak with you. You are one of a number of candidates we are interviewing for a position in the United States government.

"As I said, we are aware of your academic achievements, and let me repeat, they are most impressive."

Christine interrupted,

"What is this position and will it be available after I complete my final semester in June?"

Jules avoided the specifics of the position but said,

"Christine, there is a vital need to fill the job that would require you to delay your studies for a short time."

"What do you mean short time? I can't go now. I'm in the middle of my final semester."

"It would entail you postponing your studies temporarily."

"Are you saying that I would need to interrupt my studies?"

He nods yes.

"That's out of the question. Please take me off your list of candidates, but thank you for considering me."

"I understand that this is coming at an inopportune time for you, but please let me tell you little bit about this position."

She interrupts him again beginning to push out of her chair and extending her hand,

"Thank you for considering me."

"Please sit down Miss Spencer. I'm not finished."

Jules knew he was meeting too much opposition and had to change his tactics.

"Christine, even though I know this is something that is coming to you at a very bad time and will interrupt your studies, I would like you to listen to what I have to tell you."

"All right, Mr. White, I realize that this is important to you so, of course, I'll listen to what you have to say."

"Christine, since this a government position, what I'm going to tell you now must remain between us. That's imperative."

Now she just wanted to leave and so she agreed,

"This assignment reports directly to the War Department of the United States government. All of the employees of this department are working in a secret capacity.

"Christine, your government needs your help."

"What? How in the world would you want my help? How can I possibly have anything that the government would want?"

"You possess certain qualities that are exceptional. These qualities are a perfect match for an assignment we have of great importance."

"What are you talking about? Please explain what you want from me."

"I know that you feel safe in this wonderful country and are probably unaware of what is happening on the other side of the world."

"I'm not unaware, but yes, there is a lot I don't know about."

"You know that Adolf Hitler has occupied by force, most of Western Europe. In the pursuit of even more deadly weaponry, he has brilliant scientists developing lethal rockets. These rockets, if they become operational, could threaten England and possibly the United States."

"Where would I come in? I don't understand."

"Since this is top secret I cannot make you privy to any of the details until you have signed a confidentiality agreement."

"I'm not signing anything."

Jules was resolute in making this happen.

"I know Christine, if you became aware of everything that is at stake, I would not have to cajole you into acceptance. I am sure you would want to help your country in any way you could."

"I'm sorry, I won't."

At this point Jules voice became more authoritative.

"Listen Miss Spencer, listen carefully for what I'm going to tell you, and understand that I can make it happen."

Jules did not even wait for her to grasp what he was saying,

"I didn't want to have to threaten you but if necessary I will. We will have to,…"

In a hoarse voice she interrupts him and says,

"What kind of threat are you talking about?"

"We will arrest your parents with a charge of spying for Germany. Since they are German, they could be suspected and held in prison.

"This is how important your job is, and we will do whatever it takes to see that you participate and do your duty as an American."

Now he waited for her to swallow his words and respond,

Her head and heart were swimming. "Could they do this? What if they could?" As soon as she asked herself she knew, they could and worst of all, they would.

"What do you want me to say? What choice do I have?"

"No choice." He opened his briefcase to retrieve a document that she would have to sign. It was her commitment to secrecy and her official position in the United States government.

Suddenly she felt the swelling tears overwhelming her. She tried to hold them back, but it was no use. They just came pouring out.

Jules waited patiently, but determined, until she had regained her composure. It would take nearly ten minutes.

Once he was sure she was in control he handed her the paper to read and sign.

She looked at the words and all she could think, over and over again, "I have no alternative and how am I going to do what they want?" With a shaking hand, she signed the paper.

"Thank you, Christine. You are now a valuable part of your government.

"I'm going to need you to leave with me now. We have a limited time to train and prepare you for our operation. You will have all you need at the compound.

"I told the dean that you would need to postpone your studies for a couple of months. It's all okay and arranged. Now, let us go and leave everything to us. You will be just fine."

"I think I'm going to be sick."

"If you must, but it won't change anything."

"Are you saying I can't let my mother know where I'm going to be?"

"Yes. We'll contact your parents and you can be sure they will be very proud of their daughter. We'll tell them you have a vital role in our government highlighting your academic brilliance."

Her head was aching. A throbbing pain she never had experienced before. There was nothing she could do but follow the path set for her and trust her future to this man she hardly knew.

Leaving together, they bid farewell to Dean Harding who looked up, smiled and wished Christine good luck and much success.

The look she gave him should have given him pause. It clearly showed despair and fear, but he was wrapped up in his work and gave her a brief wave goodbye. As they walked through the grounds of the university, she heard a familiar voice behind them. It was a fellow student, who was calling her name,

"Christine, Christine. Wait up."

She recognized Jonathan Simmons from her economics class.

"Aren't you supposed to be in the science lab?"

Jules put his hand inconspicuously on her arm, and forcefully squeezed.

"I need to go back to the dorm. I'm not feeling well."

Now Jonathan was looking directly at Jules, "Sorry, is there anything I can do?"

From the moment she heard Jonathan's voice she played her response in her head. Could she say anything that could end her misery? Would it matter? Would her mother be in danger? She could not take the chance.

"No, no. Thank you Jonathan. I will be fine. See you soon."

They continued to walk through the university, and outside to a waiting car which quickly led Christine to the unknown.

JOE'S WORK BEGINS

CHAPTER EIGHT

Joe was securing the lock on his final piece of luggage. He was ready to leave for the airport, and arrive first in England for briefing, and then to Germany and Marta Brauer.

He knew that she was anticipating his arrival and her impatience to leave Germany. He would need to pacify her anxiety as well as convince her to play her role in the introduction of Christine Spencer to Emil Brandt.

Matthews knew she was in love with Brandt and it would make her arduous role even more difficult. Joe would need to manage her emotionally as well as perhaps physically.

Now, concentrating on the present, he still had about twenty minutes before he needed to leave and so he opened the envelope he had taken from his smallest piece of luggage and began to read the six typewritten pages on the status of Miss Christine Spencer. He then sat at the desk and prepared a note to Jules saying, "Jules, seems you made the right choice. Keep me informed through necessary channels. Need to know step-by-step progress. Hope we're not making a mistake by not using a professional."

After finishing the note to Jules and securing it in the envelope marked for Jules 'eyes only', he categorically thought to himself,

"I hope this is going to work."

Now, he was prepared to leave. As he walked to the door, he could feel the need for a pill. He was concerned that too many pills would affect his thinking and so he just tried to ignore the pain and go about his business.

He stepped into the elevator moments later and before leaving the hotel, he stopped at the bar and drank a glass of milk. It helped to relieve his distress.

As he entered the waiting car, he gave the envelope to the driver earmarked for Jules White.

As Joe rode along to the airport, his thoughts turned to his future assignment, and in particular Marta Brauer. What is the role I need to play with her? "Am I a friend? Am I a lover?"

He knew the latter role would best fit his nature since he loved women. They would be spending weeks together and an intimate relationship would relieve her tension and possibly her longing for Emil Brandt.

He also thought about how difficult it was for him not to be in control of every operative's role.

He certainly understood that his colleagues were more than competent under any circumstances, but his not being able to participate in every facet always made him uneasy and added to his stress level.

He prayed that Christine's training would prepare her for the ordeal ahead.

CHRISTINE'S TRAINING
BEGINS

CHAPTER NINE

For the first part of the trip, Jules was deliberately quiet to allow Christine time to compose herself. For Christine, the journey seemed like forever until Jules, breaking the silence, said,

"I owe you an explanation of your forthcoming assignment."

She, still in a state of shock, looked at him with a glance of pure bewilderment,

"An assignment? You owe me an explanation of how you are changing my life. You have pulled me out of school, you will not let me speak to my mother and now you want to tell me about an assignment. I don't want to hear it."

Jules responded to her in a more measured tone,

"I hear you, I really do Christine. If time were on our side, I would have handled this whole thing differently. I really believe that if I give you more information about your role it will start to ease your anxiety."

His voice was beginning to ease her agitation and she was able to allow herself to hear what he had to say.

"Ok, Mr. White. I'm listening."

"You are going to meet a very important scientist."

Hearing the word scientist, she began to comprehend why she would be chosen for this project. She experienced a sense of comfort since it was in her field.

"So, who is this person and what am I needed to do?"

"His name is Emil Brandt and he's a brilliant Theoretical Physicist. We want you to try to form a relationship with him in order to gather important information.

She looks at him in total disbelief as he continues talking,

"We want you to captivate him. As you spend time with him, you will get to know his work habits. Hopefully, as your relationship develops you will be invited to his home where it will be your opportunity to read his findings."

At this point Christine begins to laugh hysterically as tears dripped down her face.

A little frightened at her reaction Jules realizes he went too fast. He inwardly chided himself for mishandling this very critical situation. He thinks to himself, "Somehow I must calm her down and soften my approach."

Now in soft tones he says,

"Christine, please forgive me and allow me to tell you how important you are to our government."

After a few minutes, she calms down and makes a valiant effort to listen to what he has to say.

"Christine, this scientist whom we want you to meet is on the brink of developing a terrifying weapon. All other avenues were explored and we have come to engage you in this noble effort. We truly believe you are the only one capable of carrying out this assignment."

"You are making extraordinary assumptions. You are expecting him to be attracted to me, you believe I'm going to be invited to his home and there be able to see and read his scientific work?"

"Nothing is certain but we have to try. It's that important."

She could not believe what she was hearing, what she would actually have to do.

Sheer determination kept her together,

"So what you're saying is that you want me to be a spy. Right?"

"Yes."

"You want me to spy? Until today, a student, in a university, having been nurtured and cared for all my life and never having gone anywhere. I've lived in a small cloistered world. What in heaven makes you think I can do this?"

"Because we're going to teach you how. That is the reason you're being brought to this compound."

She closed her eyes and allowed her head to fall back against the seat.

Nothing more was said for the rest of the trip. He then had the opportunity to look at her more closely. Her hair reflected the sun that was shining through the opened window. It seemed a mix of bronze and blond that gave it a great luster. Her skin tone was light and yet contrasted with her hair. It seemed flawless in the daylight.

After sometime Jules said softly,

"Christine, we have arrived at our destination."

Turning her head as they drove into the compound, she saw two high steel gates close behind them, with two uniformed soldiers standing in strict attention.

As she stepped out of the car, she saw a middle-aged woman approaching her with a welcoming smile,

"Hello Christine. My name is Edith Remson. I am sure you must be exhausted from your trip. Please come with me and I will show you to your room. There is a good selection of clothing we have purchased for you and anything else you might need."

Christine barely responded as she followed Miss Remson to the second floor, down the hallway and to her room. As she entered, she could see that the room was not stark but decorated in pale colors with a single bed, dresser, night table and desk.

Going to the closet Miss Remson showed her the clothing and then to the dresser where she saw it was filled with everything from underwear to pajamas.

"I will be sending you a tray of food since the hour is late. Starting tomorrow, you can have your meals in our dining room on the main floor. As you can see, you have a private bathroom that also has what you need. Goodnight, Christine. There's a wakeup call at 7:00am for breakfast."

She walked out silently closing the door behind her. Christine was alone for the first time today, alone to feel the sickening sensation of her situation. She fell onto the bed with the hail of sobbing sounds. The thought that this was happening struck her as shocking news over and over again. How could she be here in this place? How could they want her to be a spy? How could she ever be able to go through with this horror?

She remembered that Jules White had told her she would be seeing their psychiatrist on her first day. A thought sprang into her consciousness; this could be her chance to explain to someone who will listen how wrong she is for this job. She felt her breathing coming back with the thought that maybe there was a way to stop this.

She went into the bathroom to undress and take a shower, wash away the day with plenty of soap and hot water.

She must have finally fallen asleep for a few hours when she heard the wakeup call and the beginning of her first day. A bit groggy from not getting her usual rest she prepared herself and went downstairs to the dining room. There were quite a few people sitting around tables of four each and she sat at one with two other women and one man.

As she was eating and not really speaking to anyone she was handed a note that gave her a room number on the first floor and a time to appear. It said 8:30am and it was now 8:15am.

Off she went to the written room number, knocked, heard a 'come in', opened the door and saw a man of about fifty sitting at a desk.

"Come and sit down, Christine. My name is Doctor Fleming. I'd like to speak with you, especially since you have just arrived and I'm sure you will need to adjust to your new surroundings."

Without letting him say another word Christine immediately started,

"Dr. Fleming, you must understand that I should not have been considered for this job. If you know what they will be expecting of me, I'm here to say it's impossible. You know I'm not a professional and I sincerely believe I'm not capable of carrying out their expectations. I could put the whole operation in jeopardy. You could tell them this and

I'm hoping they will see the wisdom of choosing someone else."

"Ok Christine, I hear you, but since we have some time to talk, let's discuss your feelings about what you've been asked to participate in. Your feelings of apprehension are perfectly normal as well as your desire to reinforce that you are not here voluntarily. You have convinced yourself that since you're not a professional it would be a mistake to involve you. Again, these are justified feelings.

"Here is some water. Please take a drink and try to relax."

Christine reached for the glass and swallowed. Still hoping that this nightmare would end, she sat back hoping that she could persuade this doctor.

"Christine, I want you to know that I have studied the dossier about you in fervent detail. I know, from a psychological standpoint that you can achieve all that will be expected of you. Of that, I have no doubt.

"Have you any idea just how special you are? I must say I have been really looking forward to meeting the young woman I read about. To possess all your qualities is truly amazing.

"Please Christine, do not rush to judgment. We will meet to talk about anything you wish. Any fears and doubts you have. I can assure you that once your training begins, as well as our sessions, you will know that you are a professional and most importantly, aiding your country at this momentous juncture in time."

She still wanted to try to convince him to speak to anyone who would release her. As soon as she started to speak,

"I hear what you're saying, but I still don't think it's in the best interest of the government to invest such responsibility in an amateur."

She wanted to keep going, but the doctor, not saying anything while she was speaking, held up his hand, "Christine, let's stop here and you should go to your room. Please, dear, go now."

As soon as she left, he picked up the phone and said, "Give me Jules White, it's urgent."

As she walked back to her room, she hoped the doctor would help her.

Forty-five minutes later, there was loud knock on the door. Before she could respond, the door opened and Jules White walked in.

"Just what do you think this childish attitude is going to get you?"

"What do you mean?"

Jules spoke in a quiet deadly tone more frightening to Christine then his angry voice,

"You have wasted valuable time. I told you the importance of this mission and your part in it. Did you think the days and hours of vetting the right person for the job were to be tossed away by your immature behavior? You must do what you signed on to do or there will be consequences."

She began to reply, but he turned around and left the room slamming the door.

Smashing her fists against the wall, she screamed aloud.

"What a fool I am to think that they would send me home. If I don't do everything they want me to......they're not going to send me home...they're going to kill me.

"Of course. No one will know. My mother thinks I am going away. I have no idea what they actually told her. The dean knows I won't be back for months."

Fear has left her trembling and sick. As the clock clicked away, the next hours her fear started to turn to hatred for what they had done to her. She will use the hatred as a weapon against her enemies.

Training begins.

The next few days were a whirlwind of tests for her. Complete physical from head to toe, eye test – did she need glasses? Could she see well at night? How well could her eyes adjust to darkness? Then, importantly, her hearing – was she startled at the backfiring of a car? What about a pistol shot? (They taught her not to react.)

She met every day with the psychiatrist. Sometimes he asked her to 'express' her feelings, feelings she believed she could keep bottled within. At other times, he set up a staged confrontation to test her ability to respond to a multitude of situations that she might encounter. At times, his directness was so intense that it was all she could do to hold back the tears. Always drained at the end of the day she collapsed onto her bed.

Little by little, the old Christine began to fade away and a new woman was forming. Always before, she hid her body under loose clothing that did not reveal her lovely figure. Now, a new sensuous beauty, like a butterfly from a cocoon began to emerge. Her head held high, her back straight; she walked with an air of confidence.

She was taught to smile when encountering the enemy, hiding her instincts to kill.

Then, one of the most difficult sessions for a cerebral girl, who had spent a lifetime studying.

The physical workout; walking, then walking faster, longer, up hills, down slippery slopes, then sprinting, running, strengthening her arms, climbing, learning how to jump over obstacles.

She was introduced to stealth. How to enter a room in absolute silence, how to read lips, to hear whispers. Be aware of everything around you. Observe, remember, store information in your mind.

Always at the end of the day, her session concluded with Dr. Fleming. He felt the time was right to reveal the reason for her having been chosen for this most imperative undertaking.

"Christine, I know through our conversations that you are fluent in the German language. Emil Brandt, your target resides in Berlin, which is to be your destination."

After a moment of silence, Christine realizes that this is why she was chosen.

The new Christine accepts the doctor's words with complete composure.

"So that's it, that's why I was chosen?"

Her old life had slowly begun to disappear, and it was almost like a dream. The week before she was leaving for England she had received more intense training in target shooting. She could load, unload, clean and take apart several types of guns. Her ability to 'hit the target' was getting so good that she handled the weapon automatically. This was the part she liked best. She could take all her training and channel her anger to become a killer.

An urgent message came through to Jules originating from one of the British operatives working undercover in the lab in Berlin. Much excitement was in the air, as there seemed to be some kind of breakthrough. The warning said, "Act quickly now."........then silence.

LONDON INDOCTRINATION

CHAPTER TEN

Joe's plane landed in London, his first stop on his passage to Berlin. As he disembarked, a casually dressed man approached him.

"You must be Joe Matthews?

"Yes."

"I'm Roger Bleat, and will be your contact here in London as well as Berlin." With that, he withdrew his identification that revealed he was a member of MI6. "I'm going to be spending the next couple of weeks with you. I'm sure you know there's a lot of information we need you to learn in a short period of time. Why don't we just have a drink together? We can go to the airport bar, its quiet there."

"Yes, I think that's a good idea."

Sitting down at the quiet table, Roger says,

"I'm glad I finally got to meet you Joe, I've heard great things about you."

Joe responds, "Well, I'm very impressed that you seem to want to start immediately. That is what I was hoping for. After all we have a great deal of ground to cover before I leave."

While they were having a drink Joe said, "Roger, I don't know how much information you've been given about your assignment. You will be spending many weeks with our handpicked operative, Christine Spencer. I must make you aware of the fact that this young woman was chosen for her brilliance, her knowledge of science and math as well as, and most importantly, her fluency in German."

Roger interrupted,

"Oh you seem to have picked a well-chosen agent. Have you worked directly with her before?"

Now Joe, taking a sip of his drink, puts down his glass and hesitatingly decides he must inform Roger of her enforced participation.

"Roger no, I never met or worked with her."

"What do you mean, I don't understand?"

"She is not a professional. She was actually a graduate student at one of our top universities who was selected above all our professionals."

"So, she's not a professional?" He says worryingly. "What is her training for this dangerous assignment? As you know, she is to be my liaison. We have to depend on each other to get the job done and to survive."

"Roger, believe me, she has received the most exhaustive, militaristic, psychological and physical training that has produced a true professional."

"Did she actually volunteer for this job?"

Joe responded grudgingly,

"No, she was not a volunteer. She was handpicked and persuaded to do her duty as an American."

"I have grave doubts about this. According to my informants, this is going to be a very tough and exhaustive commitment. We have to entrust this girl with the seduction of Emil Brandt. To somehow get hold of his notes to read and decipher them as well as commit them to memory. A huge task even for a seasoned professional, no less a college girl. I am not happy about this."

"Nevertheless Roger, I'm the senior agent and this is what you're going to do. You have to put your trust in us and know that we would not be sending you someone who is not fully qualified for this job."

Roger had to swallow this bitter pill from an American agent and know that he must do his duty.

"All right Joe; let's hope your decision is right." He finishes his drink and continues,

"Why don't I take you to your hotel and we can start tomorrow. You must be tired after your long trip."

Back in his hotel room, Joe was glad to be alone. He was desperate for his pills. He delayed taking his medication until he had performed his usual routine inspection for any devices.

Now gratefully the pill was within his reach and he anticipated the relief that it would soon bring.

He regretted having to pull rank on Roger because he himself had a doubtful gut feeling about the use of an amateur for this treacherous undertaking. Being trained under monitored supervision and the actuality of facing unknown obstacles in the field were two completely different things.

Sleep brought the necessary rest his body craved. After a few hours, he felt alert and ready to begin the intense briefing.

In awe of the intelligence and perseverance of the English, Joe felt honored that he could be a part of their struggle to stay free from the unspeakable alternative. His indoctrination included the technological advances of radar, as well as a coding system by which he could communicate with the British. He needed to understand the locations of those participating in the French Underground to enter Germany from France as well as the ultimate escape route.

Three weeks later, after completing his indoctrination, he headed towards his prearranged destination....Berlin.

The first leg of his odyssey was the countryside of France where the underground was awaiting his arrival. They quickly ran to the plane as Joe slipped off just in time for the plane to turn around back to England. Taking him to a nearby cottage, they fed him bread, cheese and a single egg. They put more bread into the lining of his confiscated German uniform that fit him surprisingly well, and sent him with a detailed map to his final stop, Berlin and Marta Brauer.

A German speaking Frenchman, in a German uniform working for the underground would accompany him. He would act as his guide and driver.

The route that was chosen would provide them with opportunities for short rests since Joe was with a 'guide' that knew every safe detour along the way.

The last miles to Marta's home would be on foot, since entering Berlin presented more risk of exposure. Wrestling with both the trip and his need to relieve his pain it became imperative for him to get to his next destination.

Those last miles to Marta's home and a real chance to rest his body seemed like forever.

MARTA'S RELIEF

CHAPTER ELEVEN

Marta was kneeling down facing the fire and rubbing her hands together in a fruitless attempt to keep them warm. "I just keep waiting and waiting for something or someone to let me know what I have to do. I was told to stay still until they contact me, but it seems so long and I'm so scared that they won't need me and I'll be left here."

She would remain in this state for several more days, before one night two hard knocks followed by two softer knocks; silence, then repeated once more would bring Marta's doubts to a halt.

With her hands shaking, she unlatched and quietly opened the door. Joe, leaning against the door in complete exhaustion revealed the words, "a tiny gold locket." As soon as these words were uttered, Marta responded with a timid smile. She quickly touched her neck and pulled forward a tiny gold locket.

After noting the locket, he forced his exhausted body to move forward into the apartment and promptly collapsed; knowing in advance, that she now lived alone. They had made sure that her father went to the country to live with his sister.

As his body lay on the floor, she put a pillow under his head and blanket over him. She moved the small beam of light as close as she could to see his face. He was much better looking than the other agents she had met. She could see that his hair was dark, at least it seemed that way. Maybe it was lighter in the daylight. After a minute, she turned off the lamp and allowed the dim light from the fireplace to act as her illumination. The warnings for the nighttime blackout were never to be disobeyed.

Thinking to herself, "Is he really asleep? Is he just pretending to test me? I had better not make any moves that would cause him to think I'm not the right choice. She stared at him for a quarter of an hour, and then realized he really was sound asleep. "Maybe this is really it. Please, please let them allow me to leave."

While he slept, Marta thought repeatedly, "Is this really going to work? Is this my way out of here? Maybe I will soon know when he awakens."

Two hours later and feeling stiff from falling asleep, he started to awaken. It was before dawn and even though the embers from the fire had nearly faded, he could see her sitting in the chair.

In her native language he whispered, "How long have I been asleep?"

"Only a couple of hours. You must be thirsty and hungry, yes? What can I get you?"

"Water, please."

After moving to the small kitchen and filling a glass with water, she returned to find the stranger standing erect and eager for the drink. He was tall, and from what she could make out through his clothing, solidly built.

He swallowed the water in seconds.

"Please bring me another glass. Also, could I get something to eat?"

"Of course."

She brought the second glass of water and returned to the kitchen. She quickly found bread and cheese as well as some hot coffee. When she returned with the food, her face came clearly into view.

He could see how pretty she was. The photos did not emphasize her lovely skin and features clearly. He could understand why Emil would be interested. However, Brandt had not fallen in love with her. Even if he had, she would never be able to undertake any of the essential steps necessary to complete the operation.

What Joe would need her to comply with later was going to devastate her.

"I cannot tell you exactly what your part in this endeavor is, but I promise you I will, as soon as I receive my orders. In the meantime, I'll need to stay with you."

"How long do you think this is going to be?

"I'm not sure. There is much to be coordinated and plans to be put into action."

Joe had to be near her and make her feel secure, even wanted.

Her role was to be the introduction of Emil Brandt to Christine Spencer. Without Marta and her connection to Emil the outcome would be doomed.

BRANDT AND GRUDER

CHAPTER TWELVE

Emil hated to report to anyone except von Braun. The weekly reports in Berlin that he was forced to give Peter Gruder, a member of the German Army General Staff, made him angry as well as disturbed. Gruder would stare at him across the conference table in a way that made him feel more ill than at ease. The information he needed to tell him didn't bother him nearly as much as the piercing gaze.

Peter Gruder seemed too young for this kind of responsibility. He stood nearly six feet tall, slender in build, hair color a polished brown and thick, skin tone clean and pale with eyelids heavily trimmed with dark lashes emphasizing the blue they covered.

Emil could not understand why a man who could not be more than 25 years old would have the authority to convey the progress of his work.

With a resentful tone,

"Look Peter I've gone through my report with you twice already. What more is it that you want to know? I have to get back to work."

"You'll repeat whatever I want you to as often as I like."

Emil could feel his anger building up and his resentment. He thought, "After all I'm an important scientist working with von Braun and here I am forced to report to this low level administrator."

Since Emil was not part of the inner group, he was smart enough not to question any decision made by the Reichstag. Silence was always preferable to questions. He was well aware of the infighting between the hierarchy and their positioning for the Fuhrer's favor. Emil thought to himself,

"Is Peter Gruder a favorite among one of the hierarchy? If he is I better be careful."

What Emil also did not know in these contacts was that there was a small electronic device carefully placed under the table so that whatever Emil and Peter Gruder said could be overheard from several rooms away. The man listening to these weekly reports, Hans Rheinhold, was a very important official, senior to Gruder and trusted by those who reported directly to their leader.

Peter Gruder was unaware of the microphone. Rheinhold had often assured him that his exceptional abilities gave him the qualifications for this prominent assignment.

Peter did, however, know that Rheinhold favored him, but he certainly did not suspect that he was being recorded.

Rheinhold gave him the encouragement when they were alone together in the dark, under the blanket they shared.

JOE AND MARTA'S INTIMACY

CHAPTER THIRTEEN

Sometimes Joe had to be many things. At all times, he needed to be in charge. Never could he let feelings dominate what had to be done.

Joe seemed to be able to relieve Marta's perceived anxieties within a few hours after the sun rose. He knew she understood her assistance was paramount, and the only way she would be able to leave the country. Joe fed her hope with the skill and ease of a seasoned actor who had studied his co-star's motivations with much astuteness.

She nervously asked questions in a low voice and Joe responded in a calm and deliberate pace, which helped maintain her composure. She had to be fully willing to comply with the order he would give at the right time. He purposely kept his physical distance, since she would have to come to him and there was no hurry on their first days together.

Marta found his presence more and more welcomed as it relieved the tension she had lived with for so long. His ability to make her feel safe and protected enhanced her feelings of attraction to him. Nothing could compare to the feelings she had for

Emil, but it could help her deal with the private pain she tried to alleviate.

Joe sensed her attraction and since he had been informed about Emil's rejection, treaded carefully until she was ready for him and what had to be done. She came to him on the third night, in the middle of the night, slipping beside him as the fire started to dim.

"Joe, please hold me. I just need to feel your arms around me. Could I stay with you tonight?"

"You can stay with me as long as you want." He gently brushed her hair aside and softly kissed her cheek and hearing her breathing moved his lips to hers. Her arms, her mouth, her body welcomed his caress and what would follow.

He had wondered what she would be like and he was now able to respond with enthusiasm. It wasn't love, but it was loving as it released the strain of having to play the patient suitor.

He let the next day move along quietly with smiles between them from time to time. A few nights later, he would reveal the role she needed to play with Emil.

"Marta, come over here and sit next to me. We have to talk."

Marta felt a twinge from the sound of his voice, a different sounding voice emerging with authority. This was it; she knew instinctively that this was the moment she was waiting for.

"Marta, I know how upsetting the end of your relationship with Emil Brandt had been, but I must ask that you contact him. "

Feeling alarmed,

"How can I do that? He's not had any communication with me for months. I cannot believe he would see me under any circumstances. He made it clear that it was over and I could feel his lack of interest in me. I don't see how I can make what you're asking me to do possible."

"Look Marta, we have a plan to make this happen. We just need you to follow through and then we can fulfill the promise we've made to you."

She thought to herself with excitement, "Oh God, I'm going to see him."

Joe hardly waited for her look to settle, when he continued, "The plan involves another woman who will have to stay with you after I leave."

She felt deflated like a balloon that lost its air.

"What do you mean by another woman, and when are you leaving?"

"Make us something to drink and I will tell you everything you have to know."

It would take about an hour to give Marta the complete explanation of her role. A dreaded assignment she was now being forced to perform. When Joe went through the plan with Marta her heart started to beat and she experienced an acute and nearly overwhelming feeling of trepidation for the "woman" who would be meeting Emil.

Marta thought to herself, "How can they ask me to introduce Emil to this unknown woman?"

She knew this must be some special woman if they thought Emil would find her interesting and surely attractive.

However, Marta knew she had no other option and could only hold her breath as she verbally complied with everything demanded by the man sitting next to her, the man with whom she had felt intimacy with the night before.

Joe noticed her strong reaction as her face reddened and her body trembled. Her acute reaction gave him reason to store this in his head for future thought.

He was right to worry. At this point, however, there was nothing he could do. Marta was the link to both Christine and Emil. It had to be.

Joe purposely kept a close eye on anything that Marta did that could cause any panic, but she now seemed accepting; especially when Joe made her feel wanted and that there would be a wonderful end to her present misery. He reminded her of the time she would be free, and complete with documents, to begin again. He didn't tell her the country she would be going to, but it would please her.

He was on guard for any signs that her resolve was weakening. Since he felt satisfied, he explained that he would need to leave the apartment each day starting tomorrow for a number of hours and would be returning in the evenings. It would be a routine for the present time.

This was very important now since his informant had alerted him to the arrival of the equipment that he had been waiting for.

He did not know if she would come to him in the dark, but she did and he handled her responses with warmth and desire. He actually enjoyed their private moments together, especially since it could shut out the war zone around them, for a time.

In the morning, they shared breakfast and then he kissed her goodbye until tonight. Joe left the apartment where an authorized Mercedes and driver waited. The driver was a German officer in uniform, a German officer who was a double agent for the British. Joe too was dressed in a similar uniform that had been delivered to him quietly days before.

The cover was perfect for Joe and Marta. She could be the mistress of a senior officer and in Berlin that was more than acceptable, almost respectable.

Joe's artificial credentials had been magnificently forged and his ruse equally sound and convincing.

The driver was commanded to bring him to a small elite cigar store for officers of the Reich. There he purchased a cigar and waited until the store emptied.

He then moved quickly to open a door to a hidden bunker below.

The bunker contained the equipment that would enable him to be in contact with the resistance and MI6 in England. Assembling the equipment would be a daunting task, but Joe was well prepared for this responsibility.

The cigar storeowner would give Joe the all clear in the evening, allowing him to emerge and return to Marta.

The hours Joe spent underground alone were first consumed with setting up the structures, and then working with the many reports from England to process, analyze and decipher. At other times there were hours of restlessness from having little to do. Some of the time was spent thinking about the progress Christine was making. Only then would the time be right for Marta to meet and house Christine.

It was hard for Joe to direct the upcoming plot and stay in the background.

It would be harder and eventually impossible for Marta to bear the directive, when she sees Christine.

LONDON: ROGER AND CHRISTINE

CHAPTER FOURTEEN

Roger Bleat waited on the runway to meet Christine's plane. He was dressed informally, but with great taste. His tweed sports jacket, open neck shirt and dark wool slacks never revealed his true work. He would never be taken for an agent of the British government. He was considered very attractive with a charming smile and bright brown eyes.

Roger was one of the several highly appointed British operatives who maintained a low profile until needed. He was well regarded in the War Cabinet as a major member of MI6 for his ability to foresee complications and respond with quick solutions under many circumstances.

As Christine's contact in Berlin, he was very worried. Being forced to work with a college girl for this dangerous assignment seemed doomed for failure.

However, he was very English, very urbane and certainly prepared for anything he was ordered to do. This was his country, his heritage and his willing sacrifice.

Women were attracted to him with his thick brown hair and easy smile.

Although he didn't wear a uniform, his service to England could be compared with a high ranking officer in the field.

Pacing back and forth, he did not stop until the plane landed. The cabin door opened as the stairs were wheeled over to let the passengers begin to descend. Roger observed each one hurrying past him. Towards the very end, a young woman came into view. He stared in disbelief at the sophisticated, truly beautiful vision approaching him.

"Are you Roger Bleat?" Even her voice had a resonance.

It took him a moment to pull himself together and extend his hand to reply, "Yes, I'm Roger."

While she took in the landscape, Roger instantly felt that any man would be interested in knowing her.

He tried concealing his reaction and was surprised at his nervousness when he greeted her. He was bewildered that this beauty could be capable of the doing the dangerous work that was required. His voice, however, did not reveal his surprise. It sounded professional as always,

"Christine, how was your trip?"

"Thank you. Actually, it was my first flight."

"Oh, you've never flown before?"

"No, it wasn't necessary for me to travel by air."

"Well, you're here and we're very pleased to have you on board. I have been brought up to date on your progress and I must say I'm very impressed. England wants to thank you for your help at this time of great need."

"Well, Roger, I appreciate the compliment."

Now they just walked in silence to the waiting vehicle. Once inside the backseat of the chauffeured car, he faced her and knew he had to make her comfortable.

"Christine, we're heading for the hotel and I would like you to get yourself settled in your room and ring if there's anything you need. I'm hoping that we could have dinner and get to know each other. We have quite a sojourn ahead and knowing and trusting each other is paramount."

"Of course, Roger."

The hotel room was clean and severe. After travelling for many hours, she craved a bath and some time to herself. Roger would be picking her up at 7:30pm, so she had several hours to gather herself.

The phone rang at precisely 7:30pm. Roger was waiting in the lobby. The bath and time alone gave her much needed strength as well as an appetite.

There were several people in the elevator and she could almost feel eyes upon her. Maybe they were commissioned to watch her. She never felt they could be eyes of admiration for her looks.

As she walked into the lobby, Roger turned and he once again marveled at her stunning appearance. She now had on a deep purple dress that highlighted her hair, skin tone and light eyes.

He walked toward her saying,

"Well Christine, you look rested and I hope ready for dinner."

By the time dessert was served, they had conversed quite easily. He asked her about herself and she asked about his determination to work for the government. He said,

"It's my calling. I'm assuming it must be yours as well."

"To be honest, Roger, I'm afraid my being here is mandatory."

Roger just stared at her. He would not let on that he knew.

"Oh I'm sorry to hear that. Is this something you want to talk about?"

"No, just say I'm here to complete my obligation and I will."

"Well, you certainly possess a unique ability to comprehend very difficult data as well as physical attributes that make you special. I will try to make your participation as safe and rewarding as possible."

"I'm sure you will."

Roger did not want to press her any further. He did not want to know how they were able to 'persuade' her. He had to focus on his country and this moment in time.

At the end of the evening as she departed, she said, "Let's see how our alliance works out."

It also bothered him that in a relatively short period of time he would be sending her to be with a man who would know her in ways he couldn't. In time, he would feel a stab of envy toward that other man.

Roger always kept in control and after all, there was an operation to pursue and they would both play an integral part in its subsequent success, or failure.

After several weeks of her British indoctrination, Roger was still perplexed by his constant thoughts of Christine. He found it difficult to reconcile the college student with the woman he was working with during the day. Her determination and strength were that of a true professional. He was almost in awe of her; a feeling he hated, but could not help himself. He could not avoid the continuing knot in his stomach when he thought about their partnership in the forthcoming role to be played in Berlin.

Knowing that she was a forced participant made his worry more severe since this was going to be treacherous, even for a professional. Could she go the distance? Wasn't there a spy in the United States with her attributes and ability who could have been chosen?

Then it became clear to him. There probably was not an operative with her mathematical ability and memory skill packaged in a beauty, yet alone one who spoke German.

Understanding this made him think, "Was there enough thought about her safety? Had the final steps of the plan been thoroughly orchestrated? Are all the elements of travel and escape routes securely in place? Not only after their arrival, but when the time came for their departure?"

While Roger allowed his relentless concern to continue, he could not help thinking to himself, "But she is so impressive. I have never met a woman like her. Of course she inspires me mentally and physically, but there was something more. I can't help think-ing about the deepness of her eyes and what they portray."

It suddenly came to him and he felt frightened. Christine's eyes showed a glimmer of compassion or was it faked? The ideal agent could not afford the luxury of empathy.

Getting a glimpse of this part of her nature gave Roger pause to wonder if she could carry out the ultimate commitment.

Since the preparation was nearly complete, he gave himself the luxury of walking alone through the grounds of the safe house. Although it was winter and frost was filling the air, he found the peace and beauty surrounding him along the path to and from the house. It allowed him to think about her and whether she could have any interest in him. She really affected him. He won-dered about their future, and would it include him? As he almost approached the building, Christine came outside covered in a dark brown parka with a hood that surrounded her lovely face. She came forward and said,

"I cannot begin to tell you how important you've been for me. You're not only my teacher and my rock to lean on, you're my encouragement to whatever we face.

Roger smiled as he said,

"Well I guess the time is here for you to leave and for me to wait until I get the signal to meet you in Berlin.

"Everything is arranged for your travel. All the papers are com-pleted and I know you'll be great. Your car will be waiting to take you to the airport in about an hour."

Sitting on the plane Christine smiled to herself. Little did her collaborators know that she was no longer Christine the college student. A new version of herself had emerged and her anger would become the motivating force to be the most skillful, silent and deadly spy amongst the professionals.

BRANDT AND VON BRAUN
PEENEMUNDE

CHAPTER FIFTEEN

Emil Brandt was summoned to Peenemunde. He sat on the plane with such trepidation that he couldn't keep his mind from imagining von Braun's disappointment.

Although Emil believed he was of great value and at a crucial point in his findings, he knew that so many of high rank were dismissed for not pleasing the Fuhrer. If von Braun felt that Hitler was not satisfied with his results, he would become the scapegoat.

Emil would not need to worry.

He was not at the point von Braun expected. He would have to confess he needed more time to complete the final phase. He was, however, on the right track. The project was more complex than first imagined and, therefore, more time was needed.

Peenemunde was surrounded by enormous amounts of security. Security at Emil's headquarters paled in comparison. The numerous scientists, engineers, skilled and unskilled labor were kept under such tight protection that it gave Emil a true sense of the value of his work.

Time was the enemy for von Braun. He would need to establish unequivocal evidence that the rockets would be operational within one year if Hitler were going to invest the necessary funds.

Von Braun only cared about his rockets breaking through the sound barrier and reaching into space. If the Army saw the advantage of arming them with tons of explosives in order to be used as weapons, so be it.

Emil would be welcomed at Peedemunde, since there was no choice for von Braun but to encourage him to continue his work. He would extend compliments to Emil and his achievements to date; he would show understanding that he needed more time and tried to hold back the pressure he was under. There was no other avenue for von Braun to still reach his goal within the time period and so his dependence on Emil remained.

Von Braun would not enlighten Hitler on Brandt's lack of perfection.

Emil was relieved and anxious to return to his work and thought that maybe his weekly reports with Peter Gruder could be cancelled. The response had been no, he must continue providing Gruder with the weekly reports. The government officials needed to know of the ongoing progress.

Coming from Peenemunde and returning to Berlin, Emil hated the idea of having to report to Gruder the following day.

Peter Gruder was daydreaming about his forthcoming meeting with Emil. He envisioned a secluded area where no one would find them. A space where he could express his desire in one enchanting moment after another. The bliss of his thoughts were interrupted by the sound of the door opening. He could actually feel his skin flush when Emil entered. His attraction to Emil was growing stronger as he forced himself to keep it in check. This weekly time he spent with him felt precious.

Now in Emil's presence, and not sensing any reaction that could be interpreted as encouragement, Peter fought back the inclination to even hint at his infatuation. He simply listened to Emil's briefing and when he finished he purposely straightened his slightly slumped shoulders and asked, "Herr Brandt, how satisfactory was your meeting with von Braun on your recent trip to Peedemunde? For instance, did he approve the latest accounting of your need for more time?" Peter could always separate his emotional feelings from his duty.

Emil sat up straight and responded with undeniable smugness, "Herr Gruder, von Braun is very pleased with my progress and understands the need for more time. I am very sure of bringing the final phase to its conclusion within the next few months. Do you have any specific questions about my summary? If not, I must return to the lab. Also, is it still necessary for me to come here every week and lose important time in my work?"

Peter stood up at attention and with the firm voice of authority he replied, "You will brief me each and every week."

Emil stood up and looked at Peter with a stare resembling disdain, as Peter's heart continued pounding in his chest.

"I believe I have all I need for this week. You are excused."

After Emil left, Peter emitted a long sigh. Even this negligible sigh could be detected through the hidden microphone and the sound made its way through to Rheinhold's ears. After all, listening to how commanding Peter had been erased any thought that Peter might have feelings for the scientist.

If he had known about Peter's lustful interest, he would end Peter's career, perhaps his life.

Peter was very astute and knew just how to play the game. He was a political creature and always seem to work people and the system to his best advantage. Rheinhold was his gateway to the hierarchy.

Never could Rheinhold imagine how this would turnaround at the end.

MARTA'S ASSIGNMENT

CHAPTER SIXTEEN

J oe did not want to see Marta tonight. The orders from England
came through two hours ago telling him what she would have
to do this week.

He centered his thoughts on Christine and her entrance to
Berlin.

The day was filled with notices of Christine's movements. Joe
needed to leave his underground facility, make his way to Marta,
and prepare her for Christine's arrival.

When Joe opened the door, Marta's heart skipped a beat. She
thought to herself,

"He's so early. He should not be here for another few hours.
Was the plan changing?" She had found herself fantasizing that he
was a part of her life. Going to work each day and returning to her,
the dinner she prepared and certainly her affection. The sound of
the key in the door and his presence, forced her to acknowledge
that it was a daydream and it might be ending.

Joe walked over to her and put his arms around her shoulders.
Quietly, speaking into her ear, he said,

"We must talk."

He whispered, "I'll be leaving here tomorrow and Christine will be arriving sometime in the early evening."

He purposely waited for any reaction. When none was forthcoming, he continued,

"Christine will be your "cousin" visiting from Frankfurt. She will need a place to stay while she attends a science exhibition. She will be posing as a student wanting to broaden her education."

Marta hesitated to take in his words, and felt an acid taste in her mouth. She knew her outward appearance of obedience was essential and so with persuasive composure asked,

"And she has to stay with me?"

"Yes, that's right. It's an integral part of the plan."

Hesitating again in order to control her emotions,

"If she must, but you know that this is going to be very hard for me."

"I know, Marta, but I can't emphasize enough just how important your help is. I know how hard this is for you. All I can say to help you through this is, keep in mind that you'll be leaving here very soon. You must have known from the beginning that this wouldn't be easy."

Wanting to make her feel essential, he continued,

"You are a very unique and strong woman who will be our heroine."

This gave her a respite from her angst. As he went on,

"We need you to write to Emil and say your cousin will be attending the science exhibition and would really love to meet a scientist who might be able to give her some advice. We know he would be flattered and willing to encourage the education from someone in a prominent position."

She was trapped by the commitment she had agreed to when first approached. A wave of quiet rage came over her, which she was careful to hide from Joe. Her thoughts of this impending intruder started to give her one of her frequent headaches.

Marta would write the letter to Emil about Christine, and how appreciative she would be for any advice. She would ask for a time and place that would be convenient for him. Emil would not disappoint the writer.

After writing the letter, Marta's outrage moved to every fiber of her being. She had to force herself to listen and even present a front of acceptance feeling emotionally drained.

"I have to, I have absolutely no choice." She said to herself.

Then for a moment, a completely different sensation penetrated through her. A wonderful thought came into her mind, and she wondered if Emil might still have an interest in her. She knew she would abandon any thought of leaving Germany if he wanted her.

Then the moment passed, but the hope was planted and this helped to play their little game of introduction. Maybe, just maybe, Emil just might be at a place in his life where his past interest in her would be ignited.

She would cling to this hope as long as she could.

Joe and Marta's last night together was filled with subtle reassurances that he would be coming back to bring her out of the country just as soon as the part she played was complete.

Their lovemaking seemed to lack the intensity of the past weeks. For Joe, it was his way of pulling back from their intimacy, knowing he had a job to do. For Marta, it contained flashes of Emil and their precious few times together.

Joe left the following morning in the same way he had been leaving each morning, but this time he would not return in the evening.

His new nighttime location would be near his underground facility.

A German aristocrat, Gert Truen, was discovered to be living next door to Emil Brandt. Truen, a man in his fifties, had been disabled by losing his right arm in the First World War while fighting for Germany.

His disillusionment began to fester as he witnessed the brutality of the new regime. Having seen a man being beaten by uniformed German soldiers while the onlookers were told to walk away furthered his hatred. He then felt it was time to approach the British to volunteer his services in their fight against the Third Reich.

He was wealthy and well connected to the German hierarchy. They were often guests at his home. He was in the unique position of being able to pass information to the British. The British had contacted Truen as soon as they realized that he lived next door to Brandt.

If all went according to plan, Christine would be a frequent visitor to Emil's home. Her objective was to procure information from Brandt's papers. She would then need a way to pass the information on to her British contact, Roger Bleat.

After much deliberation and studying the blueprint of the two structures, a course of action was formulated, thereby connecting the two homes. After much discussion, an extraordinary plan was devised.

In Herr Truen's cellar, a concrete wall separated his house from Emil's. A tunnel dug under the foundation would be the solution.

The time had come for Roger Bleat's role in the assignment. He would be stationed in Gert Truen's home. The tunnel would be a communication line for Roger to work with Christine. His duties would include receiving and delivering messages pertaining to Emil's lab activity. Roger would also receive Christine's anticipated progress with Emil.

His most dangerous job will be to aid Christine if and when she believes it is imperative to act and then orchestrate their escape.

MARTA AND CHRISTINE MEET

CHAPTER SEVENTEEN

T he time was coming for Christine's arrival at Marta's place. All the messages of her movements were on time and affirmative.

Joe sat back and thought about Marta meeting Christine, Marta introducing her to Emil, and Marta's role in re-engaging with Emil.

He was aware that she tried to hide her feelings and he sensed that she was walking a fine line. He noticed that in many ways, she seemed fragile and he hoped that burdening her with so much responsibility was not going to create problems for Christine, and the entire operation.

The next day Marta heard the familiar coded knocks on the door. She unlocked the latch and opened to find she was face to face with a young woman.

Christine appeared to Marta, even in the dimly lit hallway, like some luminous creature. Even with her tired and worn clothes, she made Marta feel drab and unattractive.

Christine smiled faintly as she touched the gold locket around her neck to verify her expected presence and moved slowly past

Marta into the room. Christine was disappointed in Marta's unsmiling reception, and realized that she would have to ease slowly into their relationship.

Marta instantly had no more thoughts of Emil wanting her. Marta would bottle up such feelings of jealousy that she knew she had to control.

In another room across the city, Emil Brandt was returning to his house. He felt physically and mentally drained from the work he forced himself to finish each day and often late into the night. It was as though he teetered on the brink of solving his mathematical objectives, but he just wasn't quite there. Something was still missing from his thought process and trying to pinpoint the answer was constantly gnawing at him.

He removed his gloves, unbuttoned and threw down his dark wool civilian coat, removed his hat and before he undid his tie and jacket, walked straight to an area of the living room where a bottle of scotch awaited his homecoming. The first drink slipped down his throat smoothly and with it came the first comfort of the day.

After his second drink was finished his obedient nature stopped him from going further. He then headed to the kitchen for another haphazard dinner. He thought for a second about going back for a third drink, a very wanted third, but caught himself for fear of having any residual effects tomorrow at work. His work always came first.

Sitting in his favorite chair and finally feeling somewhat relaxed, he remembered the letter he received from Marta and was sorry he had responded in the affirmative. He didn't have time to give advice to some student and thought about cancelling or postponing the meeting.

Then he thought about how Marta had once been there for him, filling his needs for a time and the way he ended the affair. He had taken advantage of her and felt that this was the least he could do.

The amount of time he gave to thinking about Marta was a short one. He just put it out of his mind as he moved from his easy chair to his bed and drifted off to sleep soundly for the next six hours. This sleep was necessary to restore his thought process for tomorrow and maybe an answer to the final progression of equations.

As Emil slept soundly in his room, both Christine and Marta would toss and turn throughout the night.

Christine bore the growing tension from the start of her stay with Marta.

Entering into the living room from the kitchen, Marta carried their dinner to the table. She made no attempt at conversation except to say that Emil would be meeting them tomorrow at 8:30pm at a small restaurant close to where he lived.

Emil's response had received early in the day. The words he wrote were brief and cold, but the meeting would occur.

Even though Marta had waited all day before relaying the message, Christine began to sense her hostility and anger. In an effort to diffuse her emotions she said,

"Thank you Marta, you've certainly come through for Mr. Matthews. He'll be pleased. He has informed me how important you are to our operation."

"Please," Christine thought to herself, "Let's just get through the night. God I hope this Joe Matthews knows what he's doing."

Christine only knew that Joe Matthews was the man in charge and would be handling the details from a distance. A distance that would last throughout her time in Germany.

To Marta, Christine's comments from Joe felt like a momentary relief. A relief that would not last long.

Marta quickly ate the food before she slipped away into her tiny bedroom to quietly and anxiously feed the unsettling sensation that was building in her.

I have to think ahead and the freedom that awaits me if I continue to satisfy the powers that could make it happen.

Even these rational thoughts gave way to the ongoing buildup of a strong and deep desire to eliminate the young woman in the next room.

Sleep was impossible for Marta.

Christine lay on her bed thinking of the next day with both apprehension and unexpected excitement. The man she was going to meet was her target for the forthcoming operation.

Christine had better plan and prepare for the consequences if Emil was attracted to her. She feared Marta's reaction.

JOE HAS MANY WORRIES

CHAPTER EIGHTEEN

Joe found himself pacing around his daytime quarters pondering repeatedly how the meeting between Marta, Emil and Christine would evolve. This rendezvous would determine whether the mission could go forward.

Joe received a fresh message from England. The enciphered information conveyed that Brandt had met with von Braun a couple of days ago and informed him of a delay in Brandt's timetable. The reliable source confirmed that although Brandt was close to a solution he needed more time.

The source came from Peenemunde where von Braun was observed on a daily basis. The intelligence to England also revealed that after Brandt had left, von Braun's mood was not positive and he seemed on edge. There was a scurrying atmosphere that indicated a revised schedule. Wernher von Braun was still his usual proud figure, but he was sighted now with just a bit less flare of arrogance than usual.

As Joe drew in a breath and evaluated the disclosure, he thought it was intriguing that this report would come through on the very night Christine would enter Brandt's life, hopefully. Was this an omen to what lies ahead?

Joe did not want to get ahead of himself. After all, Brandt might not be as captivated by Christine as assumed.

Joe need not worry about Emil's desire for Christine.

Joe would have a much greater crisis.

Joe would have to contend with Marta.

EMIL MEETS CHRISTINE

CHAPTER NINETEEN

An always prompt Emil sat at the table for three in the restaurant and waited impatiently for Marta and her cousin to
arrive. It was only five minutes before they came, but five minutes
to Emil was too long for him to be waiting.

Marta walked in front of her cousin toward Emil forcing herself to smile just enough to ease the awkwardness. Stepping to the
side, Christine became visible to him. He stood up when seeing
Marta and now he was face to face with a physical beauty. He actually found himself almost stuttering his first sentence.

He motioned for them to sit as he pulled out the chair for
Christine first. She looked into his eyes as she unbuttoned her
grey overcoat. He helped her rest the coat over her chair and then
moved to Marta and repeated the gesture.

Now the three sat down with Christine closest to him. Staring
at Christine, he then felt compelled to attend to Marta,

"It's good to see you Marta. I'm glad you came to me to advise
your cousin." Turning to Christine, "and what is your name?"

"Christine."

"It is a pleasure to meet you. I'm Emil." The server put the menus next to each one and another server brought water. "Please, what would you ladies like to drink?"

Marta immediately asked for whiskey straight, but Christine said that water was fine. Emil joined Marta with the same request.

Christine felt transported in his presence. He was so much more than any picture could reveal.

"I want to thank you for coming here tonight. I know how busy you are and I certainly welcome any advice you can give me. I am fascinated by the field of science and have chosen this for my advanced studies. Being able to spend time with Marta and attend the lectures had been wonderful. I do have some questions that have given me some difficulty and I hope it will be alright to ask your advice."

"Of course."

Marta had finished her drink. It was her time to leave. She thought she would not be able to stand since her emotions were spinning with every look Emil gave Christine. She gathered all her strength and attempted to keep all her thoughts lucid and look in control. She stood up and said,

"I'm sorry, but I'm not feeling well."

Christine stood and said,

"What's wrong, my dear?"

"I have one of my migraine headaches. It started earlier, but I didn't want to cancel tonight. Now, if you don't mind I will go home and rest."

"I'll go with you."

"No, no, you stay please. I just need to lie down and take my medicine. I will probably be asleep when you get back so please just let me sleep. I'll feel better in the morning." Emil rose and helped Marta on with her coat, "I hope you feel better."

"Thank you, Emil. It was nice seeing you. I wish you well."

Marta walked, nearly dragged herself to the door and onto the street. Outside she wanted to scream. She never saw Emil look at her the way he looked at this stranger. Even though Emil had rejected her and she would never have seen him again, she now experienced such animus toward Christine all she could do was walk and walk and try to relieve the hate.

It would not work.

Christine and Emil were finding their common subject an incredible gateway to their conversation.

Emil talked about his time at Friedrich-Wilhelms University. Christine told him she was attending Frankfurt University.

For Emil it was just amazing that this woman and he could speak the same language. Their communication was coated by their attraction, the attraction that started immediately, and after several hours was growing to enchantment.

One of the owners of the restaurant came over and told Emil that they would have to be closing.

"Christine, we're going to have to leave. May I take you to Marta's? I have my car just outside."

"Yes, of course."

He drove to the familiar apartment still talking. Finally, he had to leave her at the front of the building. Walking around the car to open and take her hand he wanted to kiss her face, but just kissed her hand and said, "If it's okay with you, can we have dinner tomorrow? There's another restaurant I would like to try." She purposely hesitated a moment, a crafted moment that caused Emil to hold his breath.

"Yes, I think that would be very nice."

He wanted to hear more enthusiasm, but she said yes.

"I will pick you up at 7:00pm. Okay?"

"Oh yes until tomorrow then, good night."

Christine walked into the building, up to the apartment, up to Marta, crossing her fingers that Marta would be asleep.

Marta could not sleep.

Emil was beguiled. He found himself pacing throughout his home imagining Christine in every room. How she looked in his living room wearing a dressing gown, how she looked in his bedroom when he entered, and then in his bed.

It felt strange to his nature to be experiencing this obvious change in his desire for a woman. "What is making me feel this way to someone I just met?"

While he felt excited about seeing her again, he also felt vulnerable. That too was new for him and not exciting. He vacillated between feeling one minute he was not going to see her and the next he wanted to dial Marta's number and hope she would answer so he could just hear her voice.

He knew that no matter how much he tried convincing himself it was not in his best interest, he would have to see her again. Maybe the feeling would subside and she would lose the appeal. Maybe he was just fooling himself.

He managed to turn off his emotions and open the briefcase he brought home. Looking over the notes and numbers gave his mind a respite from romance and he was able to concentrate for the next hour before exhaustion gave way to slumber.

As he fell off to sleep, his thoughts were of knowing Christine, her plans, how long she would be staying in Berlin. "Please stay long, long enough for me to know you......."

Although Emil could finally sleep, it would again be impossible for Marta and Christine.

For Marta the hours were filled with a burning desire to harm Christine. For Christine, there was alternately an excitement to see Emil tomorrow and alarmed to be in the same place as Marta. Christine was sensing more and more Marta's troubled state of mind and she knew that Joe Matthews would have to be made aware of it.

At this moment, she was completely in Marta's hands and dreaded any contact with her in the morning. Christine would have to display a nonchalant approach to seeing Emil and subtly remind her that she would be leaving very soon to another country.

In the early morning, thinking that Marta was asleep, Christine left a note on the table telling her that she was just going out for some bread. She wrote another note, to be passed to Joe's liaison. This one much longer stating her fear about Marta and that she would be seeing Emil tonight.

Then she quickly threw on some clothing and left before Marta saw her.

The bakeshop was a prearranged meeting place with Reis Hanson, the previously mentioned liaison who was waiting to hear about her meeting with Emil. He would now need to alert Joe Matthews of this other development. After passing the information to Hanson, Christine quickly bought the bread and returned to see Marta in the kitchen.

"You've been gone a long time just to get some bread."

"Well, there was a line, and look the loaf is nearly half the size from just a couple of days ago."

"Okay, we'll have to do with bread and some oleo. I don't even have powdered eggs or jam."

"That's fine with me."

Those were the only words spoken throughout the day. Christine was becoming aware through her psychological training that Marta seemed unbalanced.

What Christine didn't know, nor probably did Joe Matthews, was that Marta suffered from a mental disorder that was triggered first by Emil's rejection and then having to bring Emil and Christine together.

The few times they did look at each other Christine was sure that anything could trigger her uncontrollable anger and she needed calm until tonight and seeing Emil.

Marta obsessed all day with the unrelenting image of the way Emil looked at Christine.

During the next twelve hours, Christine eagerly awaited her next engagement with Emil.

As Joe Matthews entered the hidden quarters, Reis Hanson greeted him immediately. Reis had just returned from seeing

Christine and needed to bring Joe the information about her forthcoming meeting with Emil tonight, as well as her concerns about Marta.

Reis started,

"Christine suspects that Marta might jeopardize the assignment. She knew it would be hard for Marta and tried reassuring her about pleasing you and leaving the country, but there is no doubt in Christine's mind that Marta is unstable. She actually fears the operation may be compromised. She hopes that something can be done before she comes home tonight after seeing Emil."

Joe swallowed what he was told and knew without any doubt that what had worried him about Marta was coming to light. He would have to wait until Christine left Marta to see Emil, and find a way to deal with the problem. His stomach starting acting up. It did when he had to do something he was trained to do and yet found very difficult and unnerving.

Joe knew that his meeting tonight with Marta would be more than unpleasant.

BRANT'S ENFORCED MEETING
WITH GRUDER

CHAPTER TWENTY

Across the city in their weekly-appointed session, Peter Gruder sat facing Emil Brandt, and felt a pang. Emil was talking about the invitation he received from Major Albert Thorn to attend a reception on Saturday. "I understand that you're also attending the reception." Peter nodded yes with an inner smile.

Emil continues,

"I hope to bring a young woman I'd like you to meet. It will be good to see a familiar face, especially since this is the first time I've been invited to one of these events." Brandt felt he wanted to make it perfectly clear to Gruder that there was a woman in his life, hoping that this would put an end to the uncomfortable feeling he had each week in Gruder's presence.

"I think I have you to thank," said Brandt, "Major Thorn acknowledged that you suggested I be included. I must confess I haven't been very sociable in the past, but now I feel it's time for me to participate and I appreciate your influence in getting me this invitation."

Peter ached at Brandt's words since he hoped he would be attending alone. Peter's disappointment was obvious to Emil and confirmed his unsettling belief that Peter had more than a scientific interest in him. Not sure how to handle this situation, Emil just became less friendly in his demeanor.

"Peter, thank you for the invitation, but I'm losing valuable time. What do you want to cover today in our briefing?"

Peter was surprised and felt angry at the sudden switch in the more personalized conversation.

"I want to cover everything you've done in the past week."

Sighing an annoyance Emil reiterated,

"Everything is pretty much the same as it was in our last conversation. Progress is moving slowly, but definitely in the right direction." Emil retrieved some papers that he passed on to Gruder. "I think this should answer any questions you may have as to my progress.

"If that is sufficient I really must get back to work."

Rheinhold, listening to this entire conversation was able to read between the lines and experienced a definitive feeling of betrayal.

CHRISTINE AND EMIL

CHAPTER TWENTY-ONE

Emil just hoped that Christine would accept the invitation. He could not wait until this evening and what they would say to each other, about how the evening would end, about seeing her again and again.

Christine tiptoed around Marta and prayed the hours would turn to minutes. Not knowing if the message to Joe Matthews had been received made the hours spent at Marta's particularly unnerving.

She was afraid to allow Emil to present himself at Marta's door. She, therefore, at five minutes before their appointed time, grabbed her coat and said, "Marta, I think I'll just wait downstairs." She closed the door quickly behind her.

When Emil arrived five minutes later, he was surprised to see this beautiful woman standing in front of the building.

"Christine, why are you downstairs alone? I was going to come upstairs to get you?"

"I just wanted to get some air since I've been inside studying all day."

He helped her into the car and their evening began.

From the very moment they sat down and ordered wine, Emil felt an aura of magic passing between them. She seemed pleased to see him, but there was a thread of aloofness that only made him want to see her more. Christine did not feel the way she behaved; she was enthralled in his presence. It felt hypnotic to sit next to him, but she did not lose the planted knowledge that she was there to work.

How strange to combine this pleasure with her official burden of exposing his deepest secrets.

Once she knew she was in complete control, the conversation found its way to their common interest, the world of science and its own language. He could speak with her and delighted in her response and questioning mind.

Their talk seamlessly blended to speaking about themselves and her plans to attend lectures and broaden her education. Emil found himself suggesting that she might consider attending a school in Berlin, and would she think about it.

Time stood still for Emil, yet the clock ticked, and soon they would have to leave. Emil wanted to hold off asking her about the invitation until the end of their evening, not wanting to appear too eager.

Just a few moments before leaving he reached across the table and said with a smile, "I've been invited to attend a function tomorrow and hope you will be able to attend with me as my guest."

Christine's responded to his invitation with a smile and said, "It would be my pleasure."

She thought to herself, Oh, this is all happening so quickly, am I going to be able to handle this? Certainly meeting with the German hierarchy will be a great opportunity, but this is going to test all my training and skill.

He smiled,

"I'm so pleased."

Finally leaving the restaurant and arriving in front of Marta's apartment, they both hesitated saying goodbye. He because he did not want to leave her, and she because she feared going upstairs. The night had to end and did with his kiss on her cheek.

She would purposely save the rest for another time.

Walking up the stairs alone to Marta's door, she became fearful of what could be ahead tonight. Her knocks on the door echoed the pounding in her heart. She knocked again, a little louder this time. Only silence. Still waiting a few minutes longer, she then looked under the mat where she had been told to check if she had to get into the apartment without Marta. The key was there and her anxiety soared.

She slowly opened the door softly calling, "Marta, Marta are you home?" Trying not to disturb her if she was asleep.

No response.

She put on the lamp and peered into Marta's room to discover her absence. She now began to breathe normally again.

Where is Marta?

What happened to her?

Did she get a note from her aunt that her father was not feeling well and she left?

Was her assignment completed and now was she allowed to leave the country?

Was she venting her anger at a friend's house and would perhaps return later?

Where is Marta?

JOE'S INFORMATION

CHAPTER TWENTY-TWO

Joe finally made his way to his room and after taking his prescribed pills, his body unfolded, letting go today's tension and allowing sleep to cover him.

He thought about how the next weeks would evolve. How he would conduct future operations from a distance. What to look for and relay to England. The planning for the predicable went on in his mind until he went back to sleep.

What Joe could not possibly know was that a coded message from England had arrived at the hidden facility. The information received was about the forthcoming invasion by Germany to conquer Russia.

There was confirmation that the date for the German invasion of Russia was set for June 22, 1941. The campaign to broaden the living space for the German population had the code name Operation Barbarossa and would prove in the years to come to be one of the invasions to bring the end of German world domination.

Hitler was convinced that Russia was vulnerable, especially since Stalin had purged his most competent officers in the 1930's. Also keeping the Russians susceptible for attack was the non-aggression pact signed in 1939 between Germany and Russia.

Keeping a pact with Hitler was a worthless and dangerous commitment.

The English had undeniable information leading right up to the day of the invasion and warned Stalin who did not believe or trust their motives. Therefore, an unprepared and shocked Stalin would cause his country to face many barbarous battles and horrific treatment of its citizens, almost destroying their very existence.

Joe's spirits rose at the news that this could be a welcomed diversion of manpower that could work in their favor.

CHRISTINE MAKES HER DEBUT

CHAPTER TWENTY-THREE

Morning came and still no Marta.

It was imperative that Christine meet Reis Hanson at the assigned time and place. She prepared a note for Joe, informing him that she will be accompanying Emil tonight at the home of Major Thorn.

She also informed him of Marta's absence and would await further instructions.

Later when she met Reis, they exchanged notes.

When she arrived back at Marta's and read the note Reis had passed to her she felt a great sense of relief, it said "Don't worry, Marta will not be returning."

With this uncertainty behind her, Christine prepared for Emil to arrive. Since she had not brought anything appropriate enough for tonight, she had looked through Marta's dresses and decided on one that she could embellish in case Marta had worn it with Emil. If he recognized it she could certainly say that Marta had told her to take whatever she wanted. After all, they were cousins and sharing her wardrobe would be her pleasure.

Finally, after she had made all the preparations for the evening ahead, a knock at the door signaled that her date had arrived. Opening the door and facing this handsome and elegantly dressed man she had waited for made her heart skip a tiny but quiet beat. He stood there staring at her with a feeling of immense admiration and delight. He must have been transparent since his look gave him away. All he could say was,

"You look beautiful."

"Thank you and please come inside, I'll be ready in just a couple of minutes."

"Sure. Where's Marta tonight? I wanted to say hello."

Christine, thinking quickly and not really knowing what happened to her,

"She got a message from her aunt about her father. He's not doing well and she had to leave and see what she could do for him. It could be serious."

"Oh, I hope it's not. I know that she has always been there for him. I hope he will be feeling better."

"Thank you. I'll be sure to tell her when she gets in touch with me."

Only a few more words were spoken before Emil walked close to Christine and put his hands on her shoulders. She then allowed him to wrap his arms around her as she moved her lips to meet his. She gave him the kiss he had yearned for, a kiss she too had craved. As soon as they kissed, deeply, she moved back with a smile,

"Shouldn't we go now, I'm sure you don't want to be late."

Emil took a breath and said,

"You're right." He wanted to stay in her kiss, wanted to keep his arms around her body, so he needed to force himself to be in control.

This was going to be Christine's most important single night of her deception. She would be on display in front of the German hierarchy and must be convincing. She needed to feel as though she was appearing on stage and was playing her well-rehearsed role.

In the wings would be Peter Gruder and he would hate her performance.

When Christine entered the home of Major Thorn, her first act began. She was on the arm of a highly respected and admired man, and she drew on the past weeks of intense training that helped her steady her nerves and appear both unaccustomed to her surroundings and yet as an educated and confident young woman. She had to show her audience that she was the right choice for Emil Brandt.

Emil saw the Major and the first introduction began,

"Major Thorn, thank you again for your most cordial invitation." And then addressing Christine, "I'd like you to meet Frau Christine Mueller."

"Well, Herr Brandt, I mean Emil, now this is a most lovely addition to what might have been a rather routine evening. Please let me introduce you both to our little group. They are always intrigued by newcomers who can join in the conversation."

It was right after Emil and Christine greeted the guests that Peter Gruder made his appearance walking in from another room. Peter made his way through the mingling crowd and smiled as he approached Emil and Christine. His smile was slightly crooked and his molten eyes were disturbingly penetrating. His eyes took in the beauty of Christine and then at Emil. He said,

"So glad you both could come, and now who is this attractive woman, Emil?" As he looked at her, he extended his right hand to shake hers and then Emil said, "Christine, I'd like you to meet Peter Gruder. Peter, this is Christine. She is visiting from Frankfurt and I'm trying to convince her to stay on in Berlin."

In Peter's mind, it was a statement that was perhaps a bit too obvious and maybe a cover for his real feelings towards him. When Peter wanted something or someone, he always found himself rationalizing a "possibility."

Peter smiled outwardly and said to Emil, "I don't blame you. This is a lovely looking woman. Please let us join the others." Peter was on guard to hear just what this woman would say. He already detested her appearance and hoped that she would be intimidated by such members of the upper echelon but, Christine was not only a confident and brilliant 'student', she knew the art of engaging and saying just enough, and listening to more than enough. Her capacity to remember words, phrases and attitudes would be very useful to her contacts. The air seemed to be charged with excitement covered in the muted rumblings of meetings to be held in the near future. She couldn't quite figure out the significance of these meetings, but she knew they were meaningful and needed to be mentioned. She heard the word 'Barbarossa' but did not know its' significance. Later she would learn that Joe had already been informed.

Several of the women in the room seemed to be ornaments on the arms of the men they were with. They smiled, laughed and touched their escorts too much. The others were quiet and serious. Christine was neither that evening leaving many to wonder how such a lady could converse and at the same time appear not to intrude.

This was a winning combination for Emil. A woman he could talk to and who would listen intently, to whom he might even make him want to devote his personal life. He just couldn't wait for the evening at Major Thorn's to end and to be alone with her. He devoured her smile as she caught his look of approval and pride.

Peter Gruder was not himself tonight as he looked over at Herr Rheinhold staring at him from across the room. Peter was sure his lover never suspected him of being interested in anyone else. After all, Peter was superb at masking his feelings and playing the part of a man in love only with Rheinhold. Peter couldn't wait for the evening to end. When it did, and during and after his dutiful lovemaking, he would think about Emil. Then he would think about Christine with ominous thoughts about how she seemed to captivate Emil and those present.

He had to check her out, find something damaging for Emil to inadvertently discover.

Tonight, however, belonged to Christine and Emil.

After the success and acceptance of his leading lady, Emil suggested to Christine that they stop by his home. It was closer than hers, only two blocks away, and since it was so cold, a warm brandy would be just the pretense that he needed. Christine politely agreed.

Emil unlocked the first and then the second inner door to display a main room well furnished, neat and comfortable. He hung their coats in the closet nearby and started the fire while asking her to make herself at home.

She walked over and sat down on the large sofa with soft pillows she could feel resting on her back. After the burning wood caught and started to warm the room he poured the cognac and moved to where she sat. Their first sips were in silence. He did not want to break the spell. So slowly sipping the last drops of liquor Emil put their brandy glasses down on the small table in front of them. He was very careful not to overwhelm her with his unimaginable desire and so he leaned gently toward her and thought he was waiting forever for her reaction to his small advance.

Christine believed that at that instant her indoctrination had never been more imperative. She had to hold herself in check and yet allow portions of her physical aching for him surface. She remembered the role she was playing, to seduce him and be in his home. Christine whispered close to his ear, "Tonight I want to see where you sleep and sleep where you sleep".

She then allowed herself to respond to his kisses, foreplay and finally their ultimate lovemaking.

Emil stood up and lifted her up into his arms, carried her to his bedroom where they did little sleeping that night.

The morning hours on this Sunday gave Emil and Christine a little more time before his work would intervene and they would have to part, even for a little while. Emil needed to designate working hours on the weekend and would have to, even today. All he could do was wish the next hour together would slow to a halt. However, it was not standing still and now he was watching her standing there washed and dressed as he just blurted out,

"I wish you weren't thinking about going back to Frankfurt." It was all Emil could think about this morning even though Christine had not said a word about leaving. He was compelled to find out what her plans were and how to alter them.

"I'm not planning to leave just yet. I'll be here at least another week."

Emil would have to leave it at that for the moment. "Can I see you again tomorrow night?"

Christine responded with a smile,

"That would be lovely."

"I just wish we could spend more time today, but I have to prepare work for tomorrow."

"I can completely appreciate your needing to work. I believe it is often a priority. I know enough about the field to know how important a solid work ethic is. I admire you for your diligence."

Emil wanted to grab and kiss her for her ability to comprehend his world. Even without knowing his actual work she was the kind of woman that he could depend upon to understand his not always being able to be at her side.

As she was ready to leave his home to meet the car he had arranged for her he wrapped her in his arms and whispered, "Till tomorrow night, my sweet."

Christine moved to his lips and they kissed the kiss that would hold him until tomorrow.

Back at Marta's home looking in the mirror and seeing herself flushed from lovemaking, she had to pull herself back and remember her assignment.

It would be every night that Christine and Emil would meet, dine, make love and spend each night until the morning together. He would work straight until 9:00 pm every night so he wouldn't have to bring work home. He had to see her.

He was in love. Never before had this happened to him and the feeling was both extraordinary and exhilarating.

Emil feared that if he did not say something to keep her in Berlin he might lose her forever. He knew the week they spent together was not really enough time for two people to get to know one another, but with the war upon them even this short time was enough for him to know that he wanted to spend the rest of his life with her.

"I don't want you to go back to Frankfurt. Please."

"I don't know how I can't. I have to return to school. I cannot afford to stay here by myself and continue my education."

"You could if you lived," and then with a pang in his heart, "I mean marry me."

"Emil, do you know what you're asking me? We've only known each other a week, how can you be so sure?"

"All I can say is that you have come into my life and I don't ever want to think you won't be at my side. I have never felt this way before and if I do not act now, well I can't imagine how I'll feel if you leave."

"I'm breathless at the thought that I will be your wife and share your home."

Emil never felt so sure of anything. He just felt glorious.

Christine felt both elated and truly terrified.

As Peter Gruder watched this developing romance between Emil and Christine his blood began to boil. He kept thinking, "Who is this woman who suddenly appeared in Emil's life? There is something suspicious about the timing, and I am determined to do some investigating on my own."

THE COMMITMENT

CHAPTER TWENTY-FOUR

J oe was ecstatic when Reis delivered the news about Christine and Emil. He almost didn't believe it. That it happened so soon and they would actually marry in a few weeks was music to his, as well as, America and England's ears.

He discreetly reveled at his decision to approve of the recruitment of Christine. The plot and its strategy and tactics were all his idea and now it had evolved into an operation of major achievement and enormous consequences.

He was signaling Roger Bleat with the new development, along with instructions that Roger begin mobilizing intelligence in one of the coastal branches of the French Resistance.

As soon as the information reached him, Roger instantaneously started the wheels rolling, prepared to fly undercover to his preplanned French quarters and then Berlin.

When he had completed everything and had time alone in the air, Roger thought about Christine in the arms of Emil Brandt and it bothered him. However, he was a professional and could be counted on to repress the mental picture he was now envisioning.

Roger would be secretly living with Gert Truen and directly receiving from Christine the ongoing and current data that Emil Brandt unknowingly provides.

Roger had appeared dressed in a dark German uniform at Gert Truen's house. The car bringing Roger was driven by Herr Truen's driver and confidant. Since there were many distinguished visitors who came and went from his residence, suspicion did not fall upon their callers, and Roger was able to blend in with the German officers.

The German hierarchy often consulted Gert Truen on policy issues. He knew how to ingratiate himself. Truen's past war injury added to his hero status and the advice he offered was smart, uncomplicated and politically correct.

It also gave him the ability to plant seeds for present and future programs that could be acted upon later by the very people he pronounced as the enemy. The hours with Roger were spent going over his new confirmed information on German troop assemblages organizing to move east. He also showed Roger the blueprint of all the rooms in his house, especially the special passage in the living room, as well as the cellar where the tunnel to Brandt's home had been secured just before Christine entered Brandt's life.

PETER GRUDER'S RAGE

CHAPTER TWENTY-FIVE

In the confines of the small private office, Peter Gruder congratulated Emil on his forthcoming marriage. Gruder tried to control his jealousy, but his unnatural voice was picked up on the other end of the apparatus.

"You know, Emil, this is not a great time to take any time off, even if it's for a honeymoon."

"Of course we both know that. Christine is just fine with having to wait, even months. She completely understands how my work must come first."

"You're a lucky man. Please give her my regards."

He only asked casual questions about Christine and her background. He purposely did not probe. He would bide his time to extract anything direct.

Peter sat quietly in his chair for over ten minutes after Emil left and Rheinhold could not hear any movement coming from the room. The silence and the unnatural sounding voice from Peter confirmed his lack of faith in his lover. Rheinhold felt a germ of jealousy coming from Gruder, and since he was always alert to the possibility of Gruder's other affairs, made a very strong note of it. Now the time had come to begin to manipulate Peter, starting tonight. He had official information to tell Peter and would do so just after dinner, in a formal tone tinged with underlining acrimony.

It was now April 13, 1941 and Herr Rheinhold leaned forward while they pushed away the dessert dishes, as they were about to have brandy. He told Peter in some detail about the planning for Barbarossa (German invasion of Russia), scheduled for June 22, 1941.

He watched Peter's reaction with close attention since he briefed him in a faint but very stiff manner to arouse a feeling of disquiet in him. He then stared at Peter who couldn't quite grasp this negligible but definite difference in Rheinhold's attitude.

Peter wondered if his manner seemed threatening. Was he playing a game and if so why? He always knew that with one click of his finger Rheinhold could change his life to sheer misery. He suddenly conjured up visions of being sent to Russia or worse. He thought to himself, "Calm down, your imagination is getting the best of you." He knew that Rheinhold suspected nothing of his attraction to Emil. At least he believed that.

And so,

Peter would remain ignorant to Rheinhold's real suspicion and continue to contemplate his ultimate goal of a very intimate, very physical relationship with the man who had sat across from him earlier in the day. And yet,

Peter still could not dismiss the unfamiliar feeling and would think and think about anything that might be dissatisfying Rheinhold. He worried about Brandt's progress with the project at Peenemunde. Was that it? Did Rheinhold feel he wasn't doing a good job? Would he be of value once Brandt succeeded in his part? Peter thought about the rumors that Rheinhold had tossed away lovers in the past, and all at once, his confidence wavered.

Peter, in his insidious way, was looking for a way to get back into Rheinhold's good graces. Gruder's jealousy will lead him to try and uncover something about the woman that Emil will be marrying. If he could prove that Brandt was involved with the enemy of the Reich, no one could stop his succeeding at whatever he wished.

Rheinhold believed that he had succeeded in planting uneasiness in Gruder's mind, and felt a tinge of sweet revenge. Even if Peter did not directly know what the reasons were, he would be ever attentive and that would definitely translate to a more intense and pleasing union tonight and the next nights.

He would keep him on a short leash and just enjoy a new, exciting and submissive Peter.

THE MARRIAGE

CHAPTER TWENTY-SIX

Mrs. Emil Brandt was preparing dinner on the fifth night since they were married. After the food was cooked, Christine bathed and hung up her daytime clothing to dress for the evening. She looked at herself in the mirror as she applied just a bit of make-up and then dabbed on a little fragrance. She was now ready for her husband's arrival and she found herself longing to see him.

The past few days were a blur of anticipation before he walked through the door, and when he arrived, all her senses begged for him. She could allow the breathless feelings to flourish for the last four days, since he had not brought home his briefcase.

Always on the alert to read his findings, she was disappointed that so far he had come home empty handed.

However, tonight would be different.

Although he greedily wanted their time together to be just for them, he had to go over an equation he had been trying all day to solve. He felt he was getting closer to a particular piece of the puzzle where even his desire for Christine would not interfere.

He would save the hours he needed to work until after they made love. That he wouldn't sacrifice. It was so powerful to be next to her, that their rapture was like a flash of lightning that seemed to fade too soon. It did not matter how long their private time was, it was never enough. Christine always left him wanting more.

Finally, he arrived home and nearly ran toward her even before he removed his coat. He kissed her mouth passionately, before realizing that he had not even put his briefcase down. Now the moment she sees the briefcase she is jolted into reality. She has a duty to perform which must begin tonight. Her passion for him was so great that it almost made her forget her assignment, but this she would not give in to. He just wanted to lie next to her in bed, but he knew that his work awaited him and he grudgingly made himself get up and go into the study and begin the evening's labor. He told her that his work was classified, and although he didn't want to work, he had to.

As he was engaged in his efforts, Christine, with a startled flash of urgency would go into action. Getting out of bed she went into the kitchen to begin her preparations. She withdraw the sedative from its hidden location and laced it into the brewed tea.

As he was writing, she smilingly brought him the cup of tea. He gratefully accepted and said, "This is just what I wanted. You always know just what I need."

Sleepiness would overcome him shortly and his head relaxed forward with his eyes shut. As soon as she was sure he was in a drugged state, she immediately began to go through the equations on his papers, being careful not to rouse him.

Quickly and silently, she absorbed his writings while at the same time watching him surreptitiously for any signs that he was awakening. She would replay the calculations again in her mind until she was sure she had retained them.

She was astounded at his mathematical artistry and was awed by his brilliance. She was also very aware that the pages might contain the advanced stage of answers toward a terrifying conclusion. But for now her concentration was of the moment.

She completed as much as she could in this limited time and quickly returned those fearsome documents to their exact order. Once she felt satisfied, she nudged Emil and told him to move to their bedroom. Since the sedative was relatively mild and would have no side effects, he thought he had dropped for a few minutes. His well-trained nature automatically placed the papers back in the attaché, locked the small bolt and then he stumbled his way back to bed and to sleep in her arms.

Christine however, would not sleep. She nearly forgot for the moment that she was here for a reason and it did not involve love, the love she now experienced with the man beside her. She needed to control her thinking and force herself to remember the written equations on the papers she had witnessed earlier. Her extraordinary ability had absorbed the calculations that she will memorize overnight.

In the morning, after Emil had left for work, she committed her findings to paper and prepared to go through the tunnel to meet with Roger.

The effort to retrieve his writings had left her physically and mentally exhausted. It was with relief that she could now pass it on to Roger. Roger will also include a note of his own. These important pieces of information will be transmitted to Joe.

They not only contain the results of Christine's findings, but Roger's knowledge of her unfortunate love for Emil. Roger leaves the house to bring the letter to a predetermined drop off point that Reis will recover and bring to Joe.

Joe had not realized that Christine had fallen in love with Brandt. It was not until Roger had noticed that she, although able to relay the findings seemed to exhibit a sign of real caring. Roger had asked her about her feelings and when he pressed her, she confessed to how she felt. Roger had spent an hour bringing her back to reality and the job at hand. He also reminded her that Emil Brandt was the enemy and any feelings for him would have to stay in check.

When Emil came home the next night he brought the brief-case home again, but with the attitude that he was having trouble. He actually told her he was stuck on a particular area that he just wasn't able to bring to a conclusion. After all, she was his wife and though he never told her anything about the exact project he was working on, he had come to need her! Her compassion and her obvious devotion to him. She always seem to have the words that he wanted to hear.

He, in turn, elaborated on his feelings for Adolf Hitler, "Hitler is our savior. He will be the man who will bring Germany back to its rightful place in the world."

His face was so aglow with worship for this man that she knew he could never betray his country. Not for her, not for anyone, never.

That night, after their lovemaking, he found his desire to work so difficult, that he almost let it go. No, he could not and would not.

This night when offered a soothing cup of tea about an hour later he looked at his love and said, "No dear, I'm through for the evening. Let's just go to bed." He gathered his papers and secured them in the briefcase.

Christine would have no work to do tonight, but would pass on the information that Emil was having a problem with his work. In addition, he had expressed a great love for the Fuhrer and any thoughts about converting him to betray his country would never happen.

He could never be turned.

PETER DISCOVERY

CHAPTER TWENTY-SEVEN

Peter Gruder's bed was empty that night. Rheinhold had called earlier and told him he was going to be busy. An anxious Peter lay under his covers and between obsessing about Rheinhold and why he was distancing himself, he was thinking about how clever he felt when ordering his men to observe Emil Brandt's home and report any movement from Christine Brandt. He had been having her watched and followed. He also had her background checked.

Unable to sleep he put on his robe and paced back and forth ruminating about the fact that his men had reported that no one in her supposed hometown in Frankfurt seemed to know her.

Peter had been able to secure the name of the town through the minimal background that Brandt had provided. The town was Flughafen.

Now he was convinced he had to probe deeper.

CHAPTER TWENTY-EIGHT

Roger's sources informed him that Emil brought his papers home for a second night. He now had met with Christine only once and anxiously awaited to hear Christine's evaluation in the morning. However, there would be no direct information to provide.

Christine had told Roger,

"Emil never drank the tea. I came to him about an hour after he started and he said that he didn't want anything. He said he was through for the night and packed his briefcase. I really couldn't see anything fast enough since he gathered up the papers too quickly."

"Oh, did you get anything I can tell Matthews?"

"Yes, he came home and wasn't himself. I asked him how he was since he looked upset and he actually told me that he was at an impasse with his work. I purposely didn't pry but definitely got the sense that he had hit a wall in his findings."

Roger responded,

"We have to pray that he doesn't break through the calculations by tonight. You are going to need to be vigilant for anything he might say or do. This could possibly be the night.

"Well then Christine you know what has to be done."

Christine was feeling miserable at the thought she might have to act, act against the man she had fallen in love with. She had found a way to take their moments together a day at a time, blotting out any thought of a future, any thought of anything except being in his arms and feeling the glory of being one.

Her training, however, brought her back to the essence of her assignment. She was brought to this point for a purpose and would perform accordingly.

Photographs that she had been shown at the compound, of German ruthlessness and savagery, began to fill her mind.

CHAPTER TWENTY-NINE

On the third night, he again brought home the briefcase looking as though there was still no solution. He would have to work just as soon as their dinner and lovemaking ended.

Tonight he drank the cup of tea laced with the drug and he soon dozed off. Now, Christine's work began. She poured over his calculations with such intense concentration, not realizing that he was beginning to awaken. She caught herself just in time to avoid his eyes on her.

He did though see her hands on his papers.

"Oh, my dear, what are you doing?"

"I thought I would just gather your papers since you seem so tired, and I thought you might spill the cup of tea over them. Did I do anything wrong?"

"Well, you should leave this to me." He deposited the papers in his briefcase and said,

"Let's just go to sleep."

"Of course."

Another sleepless night was ahead, full of numbers and calculations. She was amazed at her own ability to be able to grasp and remember the complexity of his writings.

As Emil drifted off to sleep, he found himself wondering why Christine was gathering his papers. He immediately brushed it off. He wanted to believe what she said.

He would wonder again tomorrow, after meeting with Peter Gruder for their weekly reporting.

PEENEMUNDE

CHAPTER THIRTY

In Peenemunde, there were various tests were being performed. One taking place was a rocket with spring-flap valve, opening and closing at a rate of forty-seven times a second.

This was the design of a Munich engineer, Paul Schmidt, and its success as one of the ingredients in reaching outer space was very promising. Von Braun worked feverishly to complete his rocket deadline for the Fuhrer's approval. He anxiously awaited Emil Brandt's completion of his part of the rocket. When Brandt's contribution was finished, it would represent a major feat toward the final stages of rocketry, and closing in to massive devastation.

Emil was hearing about this newest achievement at Peenemunde as soon as he arrived at the lab. Instead of thinking about the successful endeavor, he worried about his inability to solve the final pieces and knew that von Braun and Gruder would be putting pressure on him. They may think that because he is recently married, that he isn't being diligent enough.

Emil thought to himself, "Obviously they don't grasp the complexity of my equations and the need to resolve one segment before moving to the next.

"Von Braun would acknowledge this, but Gruder would not".

Brandt sat across from the man he was forced to report to, and felt the bitterness of having to explain details too far above Gruder's ability to comprehend. He spoke to him as clear and patient as he could and Gruder pretended to understand what Brandt was talking about. "I understand now exactly why your need for more time is necessary, and believe me I will do everything I can to relate your timing to my superiors."

"I appreciate this, Peter, I really do."

Peter now wanted to change the subject and said, "So how is married life?"

"More than I expected. I recommend it."

"You know I remember that your bride mentioned she came from the town of Flughafen. I have relatives there. I even asked my aunt if she knew Christine's family, but she didn't. Oh well, even in a small town you cannot know everyone.

"Glad your new way of life is going well. Do you need a lift to the lab? I'm going in your direction."

"Well, I can easily get a ride, but if you're going in my way I guess that would be fine and thank you."

In the car, sitting next to each other Peter thought he would make a gesture of intimacy and move closer to the handsome Aryan next to him. A slight move toward Emil and a brushing of his arm against Emil's was met with Emil moving away without looking at Peter. Finally, the lab appeared and Emil turned his head with a smile and a gracious thank you.

As he walked away and Peter looked at this beautiful man, he waited and hoped for him to turn around. No, it would not happen. But instead of Gruder acknowledging Emil's move from him in the car, all he could remember was his smile and that would be enough for Peter today.

To Rheinhold the offer of a ride raised his anger and he could not quite figure out why Peter was asking about Brandt's wife. He wondered about the relatives Peter said he had in Flughafen. Peter never mentioned he even had an aunt. Strange.

This night, Emil was determined to find an answer to his problem. He worked late into the night until he could not think anymore. He went home to his sleeping bride, crawled into bed next to her and just before he fell into a sound sleep he wondered about Peter mentioning Christine's family in Frankfurt.

CHAPTER THIRTY-ONE

The next day Joe received an urgent message from their British double agent in Peenemunde. Their latest test had been successful. Although the news did not reveal anything about Brandt's progress, it was consequential enough that there was a successful test conducted.

Earlier that day, while Christine was out shopping in her daily trip to the bakery, Reis had slipped her a note advising her that there had been a successful result at Peenemunde. Now Christine knew that Emil was going to be under even more pressure.

Emil had been spotted coming home hours earlier than usual, briefcase in hand.

Joe hoped that Christine, unaware, would not be caught coming from the tunnel.

The next hours could be crucial.

All Joe can do is wait and hope that Christine can handle whatever comes her way.

Joe retrieves the map that had been given to him by the resistance. He concentrated on tracing out various escape routes in the event that they have to act with a moment's notice.

CHAPTER THIRTY-TWO

B randt would come home feeling a seed of doubt about his lovely bride. Peter had planted a doubt in his mind. That along with her handling of his papers caused him additional apprehension.

Christine was taken by surprise when Emil opened the door. He hadn't called ahead, but her disciplined instincts quickly responded to greet him. She only allowed her peripheral vision to notice the briefcase as she enthusiastically reached out to kiss him hello. He returned her kiss, removed his coat, smiled slightly as he walked off to his study as Christine said,

"You're so early tonight. Is everything okay?"

"Yes, of course, I just need to do some work and the lab was too cold to work in.

"They're having trouble with the heat." Now to him her words seem to have taken on a different meaning. He thought, "Why ask is everything okay? He caught himself, "that's ridiculous, I'm sure she doesn't mean anything. Why am I doing this?"

"I just need to finish up some work dear; I'll be with you for dinner."

She also detected an added strain of tension in his demeanor. She wondered about his slightly sharp tone, but just had to think calmly.

Obviously, he wanted to work way before dinner, before their lovemaking and then return the papers and lock the case. She would not be able to drug his tea, but maybe when they had dinner she would give him enough sedative to bring on a sound sleep.

"Is there anything I can bring you while you work?"

"No, I'm fine" as he began opening his locked briefcase and depositing the papers on the desk.

"Okay, dinner will be in a couple of hours."

Christine worried about her feelings for this man. She thought about the inevitable and grueling task she had ahead since she knew his beliefs would never be compromised, even if he loved her.

Even knowing this her whole being just yearned for his touch. She had never experienced anything near the passion she felt for this man and she lived day by day hoping for just one more time in his arms.

Emil finally finished his work nearly three hours later and came out of the study with a smile of satisfaction. Christine held her breath at his reaction and quietly returned the smile.

"Dinner has been waiting, but I didn't want to disturb you."

His mood was so glorious since he was sure that he had actually solved an important stage of his findings that any suspicious thoughts of Christine vanished as he looked at her beautiful face and said,

"Let dinner wait. I think we should celebrate. Let us open the champagne and have some. Sweetheart, you get the glasses."

"Oh wonderful, what are we celebrating?"

"Just so happy my work is over for the night and we can be together."

She suddenly became aware of the double role she was now playing and that she must get to that briefcase tonight. I must set aside my feelings and remember that Emil Brandt is an enemy.

Christine went for the glasses and the sedative since she knew the dinner would never be eaten. After he poured the two glasses she took the champagne to put to the side and slipped the sedative into the bottle. She hoped he would not stop at one drink. She never had more than one, he usually had two.

She was now very worried that he solved the equations and she was desperate to get to his notes.

He happily had a second glass and very soon after said, "Darling, I'm sorry but I seem to be overcome with sleepiness. Our lovemaking will have to wait." Then he clumsily moved to the bedroom and after taking off his clothes fell into bed.

Now Christine needed to get to the briefcase.

She knew that the key was in the inner pocket of his overcoat. She quietly opened the closet door, removed the key and went immediately to the study. She opened the briefcase and sorted the papers in the exact order they had been filed. The next hour her concentration was acute as she fully digested the intricate material.

She routinely checked to see if he was still asleep and was convinced she had time. The data only confirmed what she suspected. There was no doubt in her mind that something was happening, happening fast. If he went off to the lab, the operation could be over. The rocket program could be activated and it would be too late.

She knew his findings contained the information that the British were waiting for. She quickly returned the papers and locked the briefcase.

Knowing in her heart that this was coming to the end she had to move quickly.

Christine's role as a lover was over, and her role as an assassin would begin.

The sudden ringing of the phone startled her. She ran to the phone fearing that Emil would hear. The voice on the other end was slightly familiar. After she answered, the voice said,

"Can I speak to Emil, Christine? This is Peter Gruder and it's very important."

"Of course, I'll have to wake him up. Please hold on."

She walked toward the bedroom trembling with the implication that this could be the uncovering of the operation. She knew she had no choice but to awaken her sleeping husband. There would be too much suspicion if he did not take the call.

Now shaking him, she said,

"Sweetheart, Peter Gruder is on the phone and needs to speak with you."

A very groggy and disoriented Emil, forcing himself to wake, moved off the bed and pushed his body to move to the living room and the phone.

"Peter, what is it? It's very late and I was asleep."

"Look Brandt, I cannot discuss what I'm calling about except to say that it's imperative you come to the lab now. Bring any papers you have. I am on my way to the lab and I'll meet you there. Come now."

"Of course, if you think I must."

After hanging up the phone Christine came over and, with much concern, "What must you do?"

"I need to leave for the lab as soon as I can get dressed."

She knew, at this point all forces were mobilizing toward this lethal breakthrough. She pretended concern and said,

"Of course, is there anything I can do?"

"No, I have to get ready." He staggered off to the bedroom and after pulling out something to wear went into the bathroom.

Christine, with adrenaline surging through her body, she knew, this is it! The time has come.

With her heart pumping wildly as soon as he went into the bathroom, she moved to her vanity table where she kept her cosmetics in a satchel. Among her numerous lipstick holders she removed the small hypodermic needle. She knocked on the bathroom door with the needle hidden behind her back. The moment he opened the door and looked at her, she gave him a loving look with tears streaming down her face. Her heart palpitating with sorrow.

He looked at her and said, "What's the matter?

She touched his face saying, "I'll always love you." And with those words she plunged the syringe into his heart.

His face looked shocked and then tried to jerk toward her as she pulled back, allowing his body to jolt forward onto the floor.

He was dead.

She didn't want to stop crying, but would stall the tears until she was safely away.

Now she dressed and prepared for Roger thinking how long would it be before Peter Gruder would come looking for her husband.

Their escape emanating from Truen's house would have to take place right after she summoned Roger and they moved his body into the tunnel. Christine would explain the phone call and the need to act immediately.

Since Roger was on call right next to the tunnel, Christine was able to reach him within minutes. He responded as though lightning had shocked through his system and moved back through the tunnel with Christine at immense speed. A rush through their bodies enabled them to get into full gear. He came upon Brandt's body, looked up at Christine with a nod of agreement and they both put their arms through Emil, inhaled and lifted and moved his remains down to the cellar, into the tunnel.

Moving automatically she ran back to get the briefcase, passed it through to Roger. She pulled in place a large empty suitcase to cover the mouth of the tunnel, just leaving herself enough room to crawl through to Truen's house. Once inside the tunnel she grasped the edge of the suitcase and slid it into place.

Now both in Gert Truen's house they begin preparations for their escape. Reaching in the closet, they donned the uniforms of German officers that had been prepared for them.

Truen's house was perfect since their departure would not cause alarm because many officers and important people would come and go at all hours. Peter Gruder's men, who were observing

Brandt's residence hardly noticed the two German officers leaving Truen's home. Only hardly. They would, however, bring this to Gruder's attention later.

Christine had prepared herself first with the light brown wig of a man. It was hard to disguise her feminine features, but she expanded her mouth with a soft material lined across her gums. She wore dark rimmed glasses to cover her eyes. Her boots contained lifts to make her appear taller.

Her German uniform was padded for optimum size with hidden sections to hold a small revolver, close to her reach. They took the briefcase with them since Christine needed more time to memorize the findings. A briefcase was always an acceptable accessory among the upper echelon of visitors to the Truen home. She also had the cyanide pill resting near her right hand if she was caught. She was ready to leave with Roger whose appearance to the outside was that of a German officer.

As the two, walking with resounding footsteps away from Truen's house, now fugitives from justice, Christine felt she could hardly breathe. She bit her lip to keep back the sob that was trying to escape her throat. She would not let Roger feel her pain. Her poor heart was broken, "Oh my poor love, you held me in your strong arms just hours ago and now you are gone. Oh Emil, my darling, forgive me. I loved you so and they forced me to kill you. I know you were the enemy and this was to be your fate and now I have to live with this."

All these thoughts rushed through her mind as she valiantly kept pace with Roger's long strides. Shivering with the cold and trying to bring her thoughts under control, she began to think about their escape. She knew Roger was watching her covertly, but she would never let him see her sorrow.

"I hate these bastards for what they have done to me, but I will do my job and remember that I have been trained to kill. I am an assassin."

PETER'S SUSPICION ACCELERATES

CHAPTER THIRTY-THREE

Peter's reason for the phone call was a result of being notified that the ENGLISH WERE AWARE OF EMIL BRANDT'S WORK ON THE PROJECT AT PEENEMUNDE.

Peter also felt the excitement that his suspicions about Christine were right. He had instructed his men to follow Christine and discovered that she had passed a slip of paper to an unknown man. One informant continued to follow her, while the other trailed the unknown man. It led Peter's agent to an elite cigar store where the man entered and suddenly disappeared.

Peter felt the growing sense of excitement that his suspicions were confirmed and yet her marriage to a very important scientist forced him to tread lightly. He would need to probe deeper with even more evidence and thought about how he might question her in the morning. He could find an explanation for the visit and he smiled to himself when thinking of a plausible and fact finding reason.

More and more he began to believe that Christine was a British agent and he would be the person to bring this information to Emil Brandt.

Brandt, one day would be his.

Peter Gruder was like a teenager making his way to the lab where he would see Emil Brandt. Not only did he have information about the English knowing of his project but, and to Gruder more important, grave suspicions about Brandt's wife. Now he could feel free to have the Gestapo formerly question Christine once he knew that Brandt was safely at the lab.

In Peter's mind Brandt would bring his papers and then be sent to another lab outside Berlin to complete his work. This was going to happen immediately and secure the final outcome of rocketry bringing the experimental to the activated. What Gruder didn't know was that the papers now contained the monumental conclusion to the ultimate successful rocket program. The papers alone could provide von Braun with his victory.

What a coup this could be for Peter Gruder.

Finally, Peter was entering the lab. He nearly ran through the locked entries holding his breath until he would see Emil.

The lab contained the usual group of scientists and engineers all diligently working through their shift, but no Emil Brandt. Surely, he should be there since his travel time was so much shorter than Gruder's.

"Where is Emil Brandt?"

"What do you mean? He went home hours ago."

"He's supposed to return to the lab. I spoke with him about an hour ago."

"Well, I'm sure he'll be along if you asked him to."

Gruder just nodded and started pacing the room. "Damn it, how long does it take to get dressed and get here." He thought to himself with a tinge of anger, and then after another half hour, worry. He went to the phone and placed the call to Brandt's house. No answer. Ringing and ringing again, no answer. "Even if Brandt left why isn't Christine picking up the phone." He was saying this aloud as some of the attendants looked at his response.

He would only wait another fifteen minutes and then he would walk out of the lab, actually run.

THE ESCAPE BEGINS

CHAPTER THIRTY-FOUR

Reis meets Joe in their underground communication system, just as Joe receives an urgent phone call from Truen that Emil is dead, and Christine and Roger have begun their escape. Joe immediately began to destroy the machines that had brought him the ongoing information from England. Both he and Reis crashed them with long arm hammers and picks, as the flashing lights on the machines started to dim. Reis said, "Joe, I'll finish. You go ahead and I'll meet you at our next destination."

Joe slipped quickly out of the store and disappeared around the corner just as the Gestapo cars pulled up in front. Entering the cigar store, they cornered the owner and to their surprise they saw a hidden door opening and a man emerging with a gun. The Gestapo immediately opened fire and Reis Hanson died instantly.

Joe, unaware of what had taken place after he left, had begun his escape to the underground.

His saviors along the way were now waiting first in Berlin, and then in other towns through Germany, into France, and finally England.

Joe would travel from a different direction than Roger and Christine's. This was imperative in case of capture. They needed to separate until the final stage of departure from France.

It was not until his first contact that he learned of the death of Reis, and the capture of the cigar store owner, Hans Milken. Milken would suffer greatly for his help and hold fast to not revealing any part of the operation. He could not reveal anything of significance since he purposely was told nothing of the exact plan. He would die, however, for aiding the enemy.

CHAPTER THIRTY-FIVE

Peter arrived at Brandt's house about thirty minutes after leaving the lab. He found his two men still watching as he nearly screamed, "When did Brandt leave the house?"

"Brandt never left the house."

"Did you see his wife leave?"

"No, no one left and we've been watching for many hours."

Peter was stunned and confused, but he kept his composure, at least for the moment, and walked up to the house and rang the bell. He rang the bell twice before he ordered his men to break open the door.

Inside all was quiet. The lights were out and when Peter clicked on a lamp, he couldn't see anything out of place.

He yelled for Brandt, "Emil, Emil are you okay?"

No answer even coming from the bedroom. Peter went into the bedroom and stopped for just a moment when he turned on the light and saw just a little smear of blood on the floor coming from the bathroom. He wasn't sure but it was confirmed when the bathroom light was turned on. The bed was not made, and a panic feeling generated throughout his body. It was then he also realized that there was no briefcase.

"William, Joseph, check the premises for a briefcase. Do it now."

"Where is Brandt? Where is Christine?" He thought to himself.

Now the search through the house began. Every speck of Brandt's house was under scrutiny. Down the steps to the cellar, Peter pulled everything apart, and when he spotted the luggage, he immediately pushed the baggage away to find an entrance. In a frenzy, he discovered a hole large enough for a body to go through.

He held his breath thinking of his future. What if Brandt defected and brought his information to the enemy? What would happen to him? Would he be blamed? Did this mean an execution? All the 'what if's' went through his head streaming like lightning. But the blood? What about the blood? What about the tunnel and should I go alone?

He gathered his thoughts before he would do anything and went up to the living room and his men.

"Did you see anything that looked strange?"

One of his men, Joseph, responded, "Oh maybe, I don't know if this means anything, but two officers left the Truen house. I know Herr Truen gets many visitors at all hours, so we didn't think anything of it."

Now the wheels were turning in Peter's head. He took a long breath and then told Joseph to come with him down to the cellar and brought him to the opening.

"Joseph, I'm going to go first, but I want you to back me up." Down Gruder went with a flashlight in front and Joseph behind. Gruder was taken aback by the structure under Brandt's cellar that was uncomfortable, but large enough to move easily.

He saw the body of his love.

As soon as he saw the body of Emil, the shock he experienced was accompanied by a wave of nausea and powerful feeling of loss. He wanted to scream out to the murderers, but he was too smart.

He motioned for Joseph to exit the tunnel. Now Peter knew all. He also knew not to make any sounds that could be a warning to the persons at the other end of the tunnel.

He wanted to gather his thoughts. He remembered his people seeing two officers leaving Gert Truen's house about an hour ago. He now thought, maybe its Christine and Truen. Before he ransacked Truen's house he would initiate a search for Christine and the accomplice. If Truen were still in the house, he would find a way for him to reveal whom they are and where they planned to go.

He went to the phone to start the search for the two officers that his men would describe.

The telephone line was dead. Joseph told him of a phone booth just down the street.

"Joseph, go to the phone and call my office number. Tell them you saw two people going down this street and describe what you saw. Tell them I have given the order that they must be found as soon as possible. Also, tell them to send four Gestapo agents to Truen's house, no sirens. You hear, no sirens. I don't want Truen to get any warning. Go now."

CHAPTER THIRTY-SIX

The ever-frightening sounds of Gestapo sirens penetrated the thin walls of Sigfield Hone's small apartment.

Roger and Christine heard the sounds screaming down the streets. They were eating a sparse meal to prepare them for the next day and probably the day after.

The sounds seemed to penetrate through the walls and all three sat in silent terror. The sirens finally moved away and just as soon as they could only hear them in the distance their breathing could return.

It was imperative that their uniforms be disposed of immediately. The resistance had brilliantly prepared all the disguises they would need for their escape route.

It was too dangerous for Sigfield Hone and he wanted them to leave that night, not wait until the morning. He would allow them time to dress, assemble their disguises as an elderly couple and most importantly extract the papers from the briefcase. They would later abandon the briefcase when passing a garbage bin.

Christine hid the papers against her abdomen and then with a tight belt secured it carefully. Over that, the loose unattractive garb of the elderly completed the ensemble.

They quietly exited the apartment house that rested on an alleyway. Christine and Roger walked slowly, assuming the gate of an aged couple, down the alley and into the street.

This was not what they had planned. They would be arriving at the train station three hours earlier than the scheduled train. They were given tickets for the train to Metz, the next stop on their escape route. They did not want to wait at the station since it could be conspicuous and so the only place that seemed to offer any cover was a nearby café.

In the café, there were groups of citizens gathering to chatter about their great leader. Christine and Roger were able to secure a table off to the side away from the talk and laughter. They ordered the tea and food they would slowly languish over before the three hours finally passed. Being elderly had its advantage, as they were not encouraged to leave.

However, as they decided that this would be a safe time to gather themselves and depart two German officers in uniform entered the café. Both men smiled at one of the groups and gave a familiar hello. They looked around each table and when they saw the couple sitting off to the side by themselves, they moved to where they greeted them inquisitively.

A terrified Christine believed they were coming for them.

Roger could see Christine's face turn ashen and that her hand that was on the table tremble. He also felt paralyzed with fear, but being the consummate spy, he whispered to her to "hold on, we'll get through this. Just follow my lead."

"Good evening. I do not believe I've seen you here before. Are you from this neighborhood?" The officer asking the question seemed friendly while the other didn't say a word, but looked at them with a cold expression.

"Why we were visiting our grandchildren earlier and thought this café would be a comfortable way to stop and have some tea before embarking on our trip home."

"Where is your home?"

"We live in Metz. The train doesn't leave for about another hour."

"What's the name of the family you were visiting?"

"My daughter and son-in-law Helga and Reiner Schienel. They live on Heigen Street in Teltow." Roger had many prepared answers to any questions he might be asked.

"I'm not familiar with them, but of course this is quite a busy area. Could we escort you both to the train? Since you're older we would be happy to drive you."

Roger believed they had no choice but to let them.

"That would be so wonderful. We so appreciate your help."

As they walked to the waiting car, Christine silently prayed she wouldn't be sick. They held on to each other walking slowly in a measured pace. Into the back seat, they maneuvered their bodies as the officer started the vehicle. It wasn't far, but to Christine and even to Roger it was forever to the station.

"Do you have your tickets?"

"Oh yes." He reached into his pocket and produced the return stubs that were carefully prepared ahead. The underground always thought of a variety of contingencies.

That seemed to satisfy the officers, even the silent one.

They let the couple out about fifteen minutes before the train would arrive asking if they wanted to stay in the car a while longer.

"You have been so gracious and the train will be here shortly. Please, don't let us keep you any longer. Thank you so much."

They were safe, for the moment.

With a great feeling of relief, they boarded the train and found two seats together in the unheated car. Sitting close to each other for warmth, Christine leaned her head against the window with her collar pulled up shielding her face from Roger's view. She had to fight back the tears, with the thoughts of the man she loved and had to assassinate. She kept thinking, "Who am I now? I don't even know this person anymore. Christine Spencer is gone. She does not exist. Dear lord I'm Christine Brandt, a murderer."

Roger wanted to see her face, but felt she deliberately turned away from him.

His thoughts were contradictory, on one hand he felt pity for her and the job she was forced to do, and on the other hand, actually angry that she allowed herself to fall in love with the enemy. "That's why this should have been a job for a professional."

With those thoughts surging through his mind, Christine suddenly turned and looked toward him.

All his feelings of anger dissipated as he looked at her beautiful and sad face. His heart softened and he smiled at her encouragingly.

The remainder of the trip was uneventful as they reached their designated stop. There was an apartment on Venton Street where a courageous family called the Strukers lived in daily fear of exposure.

They had risked their lives twice to help Jewish families before they could be moved to a safer location. They felt it was their duty. Now they were taking an even greater chance by harboring people who must be wanted by the Gestapo. They did it anyway.

Now with Christine and Roger's arrival they could only give them three hours to stay. The underground alerted them to push their 'guests' along, to meet those who would move them through the countryside and then into France.

They had hoped they could stay longer so that Christine had time to decipher the contents of the papers that had been transferred from the briefcase to her body.

Since it could only be for three hours, she moved to the fireplace and the light from the fire illuminated the writings she tried to evaluate and memorize.

They had wanted to burn the papers earlier, but since Christine didn't have a chance to truly digest all the data, they held onto them. It could be a mistake. She felt it had solved the main problem Brandt had been having. She needed solitary time to absorb the work and then they must destroy it. It was becoming more and more dangerous to carry and be captured. If the Germans seized the papers, it would give them exactly what they needed at Peenemunde. If she was arrested they probably wouldn't know she kept the equations in her mind. Christine knew just how torturous being arrested would be and so the alternative was the pill resting in a safe place for immediate death.

In the hours at the Strukers they changed their disguises and consumed food.

When it was time to leave, Christine was not completely satisfied with her exact accounting of the documents and, although nervous, told Roger she thought they should take the most important papers and throw the rest into the flames. Roger would now take the remaining papers and slipped them inside his pocket. This way if something happened to her, Roger would still have the material.

CHAPTER THIRTY-SEVEN

Peter Gruder was in charge. He was now the man who knew enough about Emil Brandt and to the importance of his data, that the assignment of finding the killer of Brandt and the missing briefcase could be the crowning glory of his career. This would give him total independence from the favor of others, especially Rheinhold. It would also be his revenge on the woman who dared to assassinate the scientifically brilliant man who would bring glory to Germany.

Feeling smug and self-satisfied, he now turned his attention to Gert Truen. The men he summoned arrived quietly. Peter purposely did not move through the tunnel to Truen's house since he didn't want to give him any warning of what was to come. Instead, he went to the front door with his men off to the side. Knocking on the door brought the response of a servant.

"I'd like to see Herr Truen."

"Herr Truen is asleep."

Peter signaled his men and six Gestapo agents pushed their way through, as Gruder and two of the men ran up the staircase and started opening doors to the three bedrooms they could see. Truen occupied the third bedroom.

He was asleep, but not for long.

Roughly shaking his arm to awaken him he was pulled from his bed.

Truen, groggy with sleep said,

"What are you doing in my house? Do you know who I am?"

Peter offered no explanation since he was positive that Truen was part of the plot to kill Brandt. And so with a voice of authority said,

"Put your clothes on, you're coming with us."

Truen thought it best to offer no protest at this time, as he was put into the waiting car with Gruder at his side on their way to Gestapo headquarters.

An anxious Gruder was waiting for news about Christine and her unknown partner.

Now he had to interrogate the waiting Gert Truen. When he walked into the room, Truen stood up with an air of indignity and nearly screamed at Gruder.

"Why in the world did you have the nerve to bring me here?"

"What did you say? You are associated with two spies that escaped from your house.

"These spies have assassinated one of our great scientists and you dare to question your being here?"

"What do you mean? I never harbored spies. I would never be a part of anything that threatened our country. NEVER" he shouted.

"How then do you explain the tunnel carved through from Brandt's house to yours?"

"What tunnel?"

Now Truen had his scapegoat readily prepared. Truen was a brilliant tactician, and he purposely had developed a relationship with the high placed and cunning Wolfgang Volgner to be manipulated at the right time. This had involved invitations to Truen's home, with the lure of providing Volgner with carefully selected bits of information.

Since Volgner, a loyal German, would stop at nothing to further his success, there were many who feared his ambition. Truen would be in the position to ply him with his best brandy after dinner and then encourage him to spend the night.

With his manufactured indignity, Truen continued,

"Look, Herr Gruder, I can only think that Wolfgang Vogner could be the man you suspect of working with these spies. He often finds an excuse to spend the night. While we were asleep, anything could happen. I cannot believe this. Right under my roof. This is just terrible. A spy actually in my home."

Peter sat back and had to consider what Truen was saying. He too might have been a victim to Volgner's devious planning. He had heard through Rheinhold the rumors about Volgner, and now Peter could be in a position to expose an inner circle spy for England.

It would wait as he told Truen, "Look we will be looking into your account of this and give it careful scrutiny. In the meantime, I would like you to remain our guest and we will do everything to make your stay comfortable. Now you will have to excuse me."

Truen could not refuse the invitation, but felt confident of the scrutiny.

"Of course."

Peter rushed through the door and quickly made the phone call directly to Rheinhold. He discussed what had transpired up-to-date, except the briefcase.

Rheinhold couldn't do anything about his misgivings for Peter now. Peter was in a position to shine and Rheinhold wanted to be part of it.

"Good work, Peter. Just go and search out those two enemies and I'll take care of Volgner. Great detective work."

Rheinhold sat back in the interrogation room where he was convinced that Truen was right about Volgner. After questioning

Volgner with threats of exposure, Volgner started stumbling on his words and sweating profusely.

This convinced Rheinhold that it must be a nervous reaction to his being guilty. He probed for an answer as to the whereabouts of the spies, but even under very uncomfortable methods of persuasion, Volger held tight to not knowing. Rheinhold thought this could be his way to stay alive and so he would deal with him later.

Volger was dragged off to a prison cell.

CHAPTER THIRTY-EIGHT

Joe Matthews was disguised in the insignia of someone to fear. This brilliant ensemble had been attained through the elimination of a major figure in the SS. The past owner of the attire, Eric Meyers, was believed to be on rest leave in France. This afforded the underground the opportunity to execute him and secure his identification. They could not only eliminate a vicious enemy, but they were able to resurrect him in the form of Joe Matthews with his papers and uniform.

He would not be missed for several weeks.

When Joe Matthews entered the home of Herr Moldau, who was working for the underground, he was immediately greeted with words of concern, deep concern. The information about the ongoing search for Christine and Roger was now a four alarm effort.

Herr Moldau hardly welcomed Joe. He was more than scared.

"Did anyone see you coming in?"

"No, I was very careful."

"You know if you're seen there will be talk. No SS officer has been seen in my building. They may say something if there's a search."

"I understand. If you can give me something to eat, I'll leave. Anything will do."

Moldau nearly ran to his small kitchen and started to prepare whatever he could grab from the cupboard. A hasty meal, if you could call it a meal, was given to Joe. He watched and even though Joe was eating quickly, it couldn't be quick enough.

While Joe practically inhaled his food he was thinking about the search and what he should do next. While eating, his imaginative skills started to move into play.

Joe knew the resistance would do everything they could to bring him to England. The word was out that Joe could be a conduit for England. The English had good reason to choose an American. This way an American could describe, in detail, exactly how important it was for England to win the war. Could this persuade the Americans to go to war against Germany? Maybe not at this time, but knowledge always added to the determining process. This was always a wish of Churchill to find some way to persuade the Americans to enter the war. Within the next months, this would come to fruition with the attack on Pearl Harbor.

Joe removed his jacket and hat since he did not want to draw attention to himself from the immediate neighbors, and then walked out of the building and moved to an enclosure on the next street where he could put the jacket back on. Now he practically marched along the streets with an air of confidence that no one would dare question.

The sound of footsteps was becoming more and more prominent as he tried not to cause the attention to the two men coming toward him. They wore plain suits, often the uniform of the Gestapo, and walked straight toward Joe with a quizzical look.

"Sir, have you been informed of anything suspicious in this area? I'm sure you know there's a search for two men posing as officers. One is supposed to actually be a woman." They spoke with great respect since his uniform signified the hierarchy of his position.

"Yes, of course I know. I thought I might have a lead that came from a neighbor on the next street. It did not turn out to be anything worth pursuing. Now did you get any word on these two?"

"No. So many are out looking that we thought this might be a good neighborhood to check."

"Good, do your duty. Goodnight."

Joe did not wait for any response. He just walked with a strong presence and vanished from their sight.

CHAPTER THIRTY-NINE

Christine and Roger were given bicycles that were supplied by the Stukers' to ride through the countryside. They had rearranged their clothing, removed the makeup and now just appeared as a young couple riding through the wintry landscape.

Their journey would have exhausted the average person, but Roger and Christine were in supremely strong condition. This had been imperative in Christine's training and she cycled as if she was competing in a race. Roger was impressed that she could not only keep up with him, but never even asked to rest.

They traveled as dusk was closing in on them. If they were questioned the answer could be that they were lost. The rural surroundings provided any routes where the trees and minimal foliage could deceive even the most knowledgeable cyclist.

They were approaching the French border and knew there was a likelihood of being stopped by guards. Since they had excellent forged papers they were not overly concerned with any impending encounter.

"Halt. Don't move. Show me your papers, now."

Smiling obediently, they pulled out their papers and handed them over.

Gustof, the senior guard in charge, was always looking to use his power as that of a low echelon worker. After a prolonged scrutiny of their papers he demanded,

"Where are you going?"

"We're heading to Reims."

"Why?"

"Our cousin Jean Bache is soon to be married there."

Up to this point, a very bored Gustof was feeling the excitement of hassling these two attractive young people. Certainly, he had reason to be suspicious of cyclists riding in the cold winter night.

Out loud he said, "I want both of you to come with me to headquarters."

Klaus, walking over to Gustof whispered, "Why are you doing this? Let them go. They can't be of any importance."

Gustof, now adamant, replied, "I want them to come with me."

"Why?"

"Because I'm the senior officer here and I said so."

Klaus now said, "This is becoming ridiculous, Gustof."

While this bickering continued Roger turns to face Christine and whispered to her, "This is not going to end well. We need to finish this off now."

With one swift move, Roger pulled out his gun and shot Gustof through the head. Before Klaus had a chance to react, Christine released her revolver and followed suit, shooting Klaus.

Leaving the bodies on the ground, they had to now pedal like the wind. They were lucky that the areas they cycled through were not filled with snow or ice. It would be an hour and a half before the dead soldiers were discovered and the absolute direction of the runaway spies.

Arriving just at dawn they were waylaid in their progress by a flock of sheep crossing the road. This held back their progress for precious minutes. The sheep finally cleared the road and they instantly moved across not noticing the Shepard eyeing them with curiosity. He had never seen anyone at this hour, especially in such a hurry. When questioned later he would provide solid direction.

CHAPTER FORTY

Word spread like wildfire to reach Peter Gruder's attention. He was off like the hound chasing the fox, shouting orders to both the Gestapo and the army within a fifty-mile radius of where the dead soldiers had been found. He knew for sure that it was Christine and her accomplice.

How Christine and Roger could avoid the onslaught would depend on their speed and the immeasurable aid of the underground in France.

Any stop would not only endanger the willing underground participants but their whole village. Examples could be made of innocent citizens. It had happened before and now the deep seeded revenge for the loss of their beloved scientist and any documents made the hunt and capture a necessity. A capture Peter longed for with an evil look of desperation.

CHAPTER FORTY-ONE

J oe was on route when he was given the news about Christine
and Roger.

He felt a wave of panic realizing that Christine was the only one
with the formulas in her head. Knowing this makes it even more
imperative that Christine must be rescued.

Joe knew that any help along his route through France
could bring disaster to the underground, and so he decided to
pretend to search for the 'missing spies' under the cover of his
uniform.

This could give him the excuse he needed to move from place
to place, as a German questioning any inhabitants he could find
along his route.

He maneuvered his way through the cold and icy pathways,
first on foot and then securing an authorized vehicle he brazenly
requested at one of the checkpoints. His demeanor was filled with
the determination of seeking out the enemies he was searching
for. They dare not question his request.

As he drove through to the next location, he started to feel the beginning of his all too familiar discomfort. He knew from experience that the pain would only get worse.

As he maneuvered along the roads, the pain became more and more acute and with no medication left he still kept forcing himself to drive. He felt himself perspiring and then such pain that he slowed the car as it veered off the road and crashed into a fence leaving him unconscious.

The crash happened at a farm house and when he regained consciousness he found himself in a strange bedroom. There was a side table with his papers on top and his uniform jacket hanging on the corner chair.

Standing at the edge of the bed was a rugged looking man about fifty years old.

"Do you speak French?"

Joe replied that he did, a little.

"My son and I heard the crash and saw that you were hurt. We brought you inside and he's getting the doctor." The French were always afraid not to help a German since the repercussions could be drastic if they didn't. Their hatred for their occupiers would have to be kept in check.

"I took off your jacket and your papers fell out. I put them on the table next to you.

How do you feel? "

"Is my car damaged?"

"Not bad, I backed it out and its working.

"How are you feeling now?"

"I feel some pain in my stomach, but I'll be okay."

The doctor, Doctor Fernand, arrived with the farmer's fifteen-year-old son.

He was an older man with white hair and a face that reflected many years.

Joe sat up and said, in manufactured broken French, "Doctor thank you for coming."

"I'm glad to see that you're conscious now. So tell me what hurts you?"

"Actually it's my stomach area. I felt a familiar pain and since I did not have my pain medication I guessed I blacked out."

"What do you mean familiar? Is this something you've been diagnosed with?"

"Yes, it's an ulcer and sometimes it acts up. If you could give me some pain killers that would really help."

"Let me take a look at you." As he was checking Joe the doctor noticed the papers on the side table and saw the name Eric Meyers, a name that clicked in his memory. He had also seen the jacket when he entered the room and glanced at the medals. His suspicions about the name and the face that didn't match would wait until he was out of the farm and in his home where he could bring his memories to the surface.

What he did not realize was that Joe had taken note of the doctor's puzzled look when he saw the name.

Dr. Fernand went into his bag, retrieved some pills, and handed them to Joe. "Here, this may help your pain." He put on his coat and hat and started for the door.

Joe thanked him again for coming and waited to hear the front door close. As soon as it did, he almost jolted from the bed and started to put on his jacket and grab the papers on the table. He thanked the farmer and his son and told them he had to get back to his duty.

When the doctor was finally in his house, he sat down and let his mind remember the German who had come to him some time ago with a deep cut on his finger. He gave his name as the same one on the paper he saw just an hour ago in the farmhouse. The doctor had treated several Germans since the occupation. Although they were his enemy, he wanted to keep his practice and so he would have to cooperate.

He knew his suspicions were right. He also knew he would do nothing. Even if the man he just saw was an imposter, he could be on his side and so his silence would remain.

Of course, he would not report him. Never would he report a man who just might be an enemy of the Germans. The memory of losing his son in battle against the Germans jolted his broken heart and brought back the agony of not only losing his boy, but that of his wife dying six months later of heart failure. Dr. Fernand always believed that although she had a heart condition, the impact of loss was too great.

CHAPTER FORTY-TWO

Roger and Christine had to stop and catch their breath. With hardly any shelter, they found a spot where they could rest. They had not eaten now in nearly two days and the pouch containing their meager supply of water was almost empty. The many miles they still needed to reach to the final underground location in Laon was fraught with danger. There must be an all-out search for them, but they had to get something to eat or their stamina would evaporate.

As they spoke, a bolt of lightning flashed across the sky and the skies began to darken. Without warning a freezing winter rain came down in torrents.

Christine, shaking so badly, was unable to control her bike.

"Roger, I'm sorry I can't ride any more."

"Don't attempt to ride any further."

He got off his bike and walked over and helped her off the bike.

With a commanding voice he said,

"Christine, open your jacket" as Roger opened his.

"Let me hold you next to me and the warmth of our bodies together will help keep you warm."

After just a moment's hesitation, she opened her jacket and he wrapped his arms around her as he pressed his body against hers.

His breath on her neck gave her an unexpected feeling of arousal and she was impervious to the icy rain.

He loved the feeling of her body next to his, but knew this was not the right time for any display of passion. After a few minutes he asked, "If you're feeling better now we need to move on."

He knew he had to find shelter quickly or they would die here in the woods.

"Look try and walk alongside the bicycle. We just cannot leave them here to be found.

"Do not worry, we will look for refuge."

She moved the bike alongside her and all he could say was,

"You're doing fine."

"Well, Roger, we're in this together and whatever happens I'm really happy you're my partner."

After what seemed like hours a very quiet Christine said, "I think I see a cottage ahead."

The rain was easing up, but they were still drenched. Christine thought she could never be able to overcome the aching of cold and wet cloth covering her, but she did.

There was a light in the window as she looked at Roger, "Let me be the one to knock. Since I'm a woman it will be less threatening."

"I'll be right next to you Christine." He felt for his gun. If he had to kill him, there could be no other way.

Christine went to the door and knocked.

A couple of seconds later it opened and they saw a middle aged man holding a rifle pointed at them.

He said in French, "What do you want?"

Since Christine only spoke a little French, Roger showed himself clearly and said,

"Please, could you help us." Pointing to the bikes, "We've been riding our bikes through the woods and we're lost. We have not eaten for over a day and as you can see we're very wet and cold from the rain."

The stranger turned his face to Christine, "Miss, can't you speak French?" Christine was left with no choice but to respond to him in English and hope that he was just what he seemed to be, a true Frenchman.

In English she said,

"My name is Christine. Messer, do you speak English?"

"A little."

"Please help us."

He lowered his rifle and his hardened face began to soften.

"My name is Jean Marche."

In broken English he said, "Come inside and you can tell me why you're here."

Christine's instincts were right, he could be trusted.

CHAPTER FORTY-THREE

While Christine and Roger were able to catch their breath for a spell, Peter Gruder was making his way with the Gestapo at his side.

Since Gruder was unsure of the direction that the two escapees had taken, he had his men spread out. One agent came across the shepherd and received some very interesting information about a couple on bicycles. They were very anxious for his sheep to pass as they all too eagerly sped across the road and into the wooded area.

The hunt was on, and Gruder rushed to the area sure that it was their latest destination for Christine and her fellow spy. He wanted her to see his face as the arrest and interrogation commenced.

The feverish search seemed to spread across France. Even suspecting it was in the direction of where the shepherd saw an unknown couple, the Germans needed to find their enemy. They pursued without boundaries.

A house-to-house penetration created an almost hysterical atmosphere among the already frightened civilian population.

Without any guise of acceptable human behavior, every home was descended upon.

The few that were part of the resistance held their breath with the hope that Christine and Roger would not seek refuge at their location. That feeling was only of the moment and each member knew they would have to give up their life to support their country's freedom.

CHAPTER FORTY-FOUR

Two SS Officers were finding their way to a farmhouse. Inside the farmer and his son explained that they had not seen a couple on bicycles.

They did mention that an SS Officer had crashed his car and they brought him in to care for him. They even mentioned that his son went out and summoned a doctor who examined him and then gave him pills.

"What was the name of the officer?"

The father looked at his son and they both shrugged, "We don't know."

"What did he look like?"

"Well, he was average height. He had dark brown hair and dark eyes. What about your son, is there anything you want to add?"

"I think he had a scar on his cheek but I could be wrong. He was hurt from the crash and it could have been some blood that dried."

The farmer added,

"I did see some papers that fell out of his jacket when we helped him to the bed. I put them on the table next to him. You know I think the doctor noticed them. Maybe he knows."

"What's the doctor's name and where does he live?"

"Dr. Fernand on Chappeau Street. It's just down the lane."

Without saying anything more they left.

"Gee son, I hope we haven't put him in any trouble."

The two SS Officers banged on the door of the doctor's house. Dr. Fernand was almost through treating a patient, but he stopped, excused himself and opened the front door.

Outside were two SS Officers who immediately pushed their way in.

"We understand you treated a German officer at the Felais farmhouse a few hours ago."

"Yes, I did. I always treat the Germans who need my help."

"The farmer tells us that you saw some papers of the officer on the table and looked at them. What was the name on the paper?"

"I just glanced and didn't really look closely."

"Now think. What was the name?"

"I have a patient who is just about ready to leave. Maybe I should tell her to go."

One agent walked with him into the examining room as he told the patient she was finished and could leave. Once she left, he continued to press the doctor.

"Now, what was the name?"

For fear the farmer had already disclosed the name,

"I think it said Eric Meyers."

The other agent jumped in, "What, what name did you say?"

"Eric Meyers."

"I know him. I know him well, and he does not fit the description the farmer gave us. He doesn't have dark hair and eyes; he's blond and has light eyes."

"I'm sorry, maybe I'm wrong but that's what I think I saw."

The two agents started whispering to each other about Eric Meyers. Suddenly, the thrust of their search had taken even a darker turn. This had to be reported immediately, while they continued with their search for the two spies.

As they walked out the officer said,

"Don't think of going anywhere, we'll be back."

As soon as they left he walked to the front door, looked out to be sure they were gone, and locked the door.

Then Dr. Fernand, a dedicated member of the resistance since his wife died, went to the rear of his house where there was a locked room. He took the key and opened it, went to the equipment at the far end and began a coded message. The doctor warned the underground that someone posing as SS Officer Eric Meyers was under the scrutiny of the Gestapo.

Gruder received word from the SS Officers questioning the doctor, that there was an unknown man posing as SS Officer Eric Meyers. The report included a description given by both the farmer and the doctor.

Peter is confused. He must think now. Who was the man? Is there a connection to Christine and her accomplice? Did he stumble onto a conspiracy?

He is thrilled.

Could this have anything to do with the man who disappeared into the cigar store?

Could the damaged equipment in the basement of the store have something to do with this imposter?

Peter's excitement almost overwhelmed him.

This was too much for Gruder to coordinate, but he would anyhow. He would prove his superior skills and bring all the enemies under his control.

Peter, with his cunning mindset, had to think through the best way to manipulate the situation to his advantage.

He was now flushed with inner glory that Rheinhold had decided to interrogate Volgner while he was given this task; the more important task.

CHAPTER FORTY-FIVE

Roger agreed with Christine that Jean Marche could be trusted. They needed this man to help them, and so Roger spoke to him in French,

"Messr. Marche, we cannot begin to thank you for what you're doing. I'm going to confide in you since I believe we want the same thing. We are working for the British and the Americans to help your country end the German occupation. We are hoping to get to the people who will help us get out of the country. The people we need to reach work for the underground and risk their lives every day. These are your people. They want to help us leave for England with information for the British and the Americans."

In French with a smile,

"What can I do to help you?"

A deep sigh from Roger as he continued,

"Some dry clothing would be wonderful."

Divesting themselves of their wet garments revealed the papers that had been hidden against Roger's chest. Fortunately, they were still legible.

Dressed in old clothing that the Frenchman provided, Christine said, "I need time to digest these formulas," moving to the warmth of the fireplace.

All was quiet as Christine concentrated, absorbed and retained the all-important work that von Braun had been waiting for.

Finally, after some time passed, she nodded her head and said to Roger,

"We can now burn the pages."

Roger took her hand and together they threw them into the embers and watched them disappear.

"Messer, we need to rest for a short time and then we'll leave."

"I don't think you can ride your bicycles. You told me you were on your way to the town of Amiens and it's too far to walk. It will take forever. I have an old truck I use when going to the city. I will drive you."

"Are you sure? We don't want you to get into any trouble."

"I am a proud Frenchman. I was not able to serve my country because of my age. You have given me a chance to do something for my country and my countrymen. I am at your service and do so with pride."

Two hours later after hiding the bikes in the barn under the hay, they squeezed into his truck and were heading west.

CHAPTER FORTY-SIX

Interrupting his interrogation of Volger, Rheinhold re-read the very significant message. Volger could wait, but not the message and what he himself would do.

It clearly said that there was someone masquerading as SS Officer Eric Meyers in France. In the same message, there was still no capture of Christine Brandt and her accomplice.

There was also mention that Peter Gruder was making progress on their capture. That felt like a warning to Rheinhold's competence and Gruder's triumph.

Since Rheinhold was a political creature and immediately feared he would be usurped, he sent out a message directly to Gruder, ordering him to wait until he could join him. Rheinhold would tell him there was secret information he needed to brief him on.

Peter Gruder was furious when he received the communiqué that he was ordered to wait for his superior.

As his temper started flaring he received word that a couple on bicycles were seen a relatively short distance from where he was.

Without regard for Rheinhold's instructions, and tasting a victory in his path he summoned his two agents and headed to where the couple were. He had specifically told his men not to make an arrest but to hold the two suspects until he was present.

He took off with lightning speed and after two hours came across his men who were surrounding his prey. He smiled with glee and satisfaction as he approached the confused couple who were just two French people out for a ride.

Christine was not the woman. A shocked Gruder's smile turned to an evil sneer.

What Gruder didn't know was that the resistance, knowing that Christine and Roger were trying to flee France, set about sending several decoys in an attempt to divert their escape.

Rheinhold was furious when he arrived. He expected to see Peter Gruder waiting for him, and now he was told that Gruder was on his way to arrest the spies they were searching for. This was going to make Peter a favorite among the hierarchy.

Just before Peter came back to where Rheinhold waited, a dispatch came through that they were the wrong people.

Although the arrest would have been vitally important to Germany, Rheinhold couldn't help being just a bit self-satisfied that Gruder wasn't going to succeed this time. Rheinhold would see that Gruder wasn't going to succeed anytime.

He underestimated Peter Gruder.

As soon as Peter appeared, he leaped to his feet with menace in his voice,

"Why did you disobey a direct order? I specifically told you to stay and wait for me to arrive."

"I didn't want to let them get away. You always gave me the freedom to use my judgment and this was a perfect case.

"I thought this was what you would want me to do. Sorry."

Rheinhold kept his anger in check for a moment, "Did you ever think that when you saw it wasn't Christine that you were being set up? How convenient it was that there was a couple that resembled the ones we're seeking. Did you let the couple go?"

Peter never thought they could be the resistance helping them. It just did not occur to him and he had to confess that, "I let them go." In a wave of inner rage he continued, "You are right. Damn it, damn it.

"I want to send out a search for those bastards. There must have been indications to their direction."

"I want you to stay exactly where you are. You made a huge mistake and now I will take over."

Peter was visibly shaken, but still in his manipulative mindset to force the issue and said,

"You haven't been a part of this until just now. Remember, our leaders would no doubt agree with me that the pursuit has been effective, even with my single error. I have the relationship with our men here, and in the field and really believe it's in your best interest to allow me another chance to make this happen."

Rheinhold was completely aware of Gruder's self-serving tactic, but knew that Gruder would never let it rest between them. Peter would go higher and he would have to explain his decision not to let him continue.

Rheinhold said, "I will go wherever you go." He stopped for a couple of seconds, "to make sure there are no more mistakes."

Gruder could not argue with Rheinhold's obvious way to insure he would be present for the glory.

CHAPTER FORTY-SEVEN

When Christine and Roger finally reached the town of Amiens, Christine shook Jean Marche's hand and reached over to kiss him on the cheek. Roger gave him a strong handshake and said,

"We pray for you and your country. We cannot begin to thank you enough for your incredible aid."

As Roger and Christine departed from the truck, they hoped the resistance would be waiting for them.

They walked to the address given to them and gave the coded knock on the door. It swept open and they were quickly ushered inside.

Speaking hurriedly, the host said,

"Please, you have to understand that there's been so much emphasis on you that our work here is in jeopardy. I will try to help you as much as I can, but your time here is very dangerous. If you could both stay in my cellar, it will be safer for you and for our people."

"Look, we're sorry and we'll leave as soon as you say."

Roger came up with an idea. "Please, do you have a piece of paper and pencil?"

"Yes." And then gave it to him.

Roger sat at the table and drew a map, a map to their next destination. The map pinpointed the exact address of an underground contact. Then he looked at Christine and said,

"Christine, I have something to tell you."

"What?"

"When we leave here we're going to have to travel separately."

Christine looked stricken.

"Do we have to?"

"You know that it's much too dangerous for us to be seen together. I want you to read and memorize this map then we'll destroy it." Pointing to the address. "We'll rendezvous here."

"Roger, I'm not sure I can do this."

Roger had to speak firmly,

"Christine you have been well trained. You have a gun and know how to use it. I know you can handle this."

She pulled herself together, remembered what she was here for, and regained her composure,

"Okay. You are right. I'm being foolish." She took the paper and was able to memorize the details of each street and their direction.

"Destroy the paper, Roger."

Roger smiled and held out his hand to touch and then squeeze hers, gently.

Now Roger turned to their contact and asked,

"Did you hear anything we need to know?"

"Yes, I heard late last night that Joe Matthews is hoping to meet you in Lille.

Then there would be only one more stop before departing France."

"Good. Please just give us some food, and then we will wait in the cellar until you give us the signal to leave."

"Of course. Thank you for understanding.

"It will be dusk when I give you the signal."

After a hasty meal they retreated to the cellar with two candles to illuminate the room.

They found boxes and crates that they were able to sit on. They moved two of the crates together and sat side by side.

"Christine, why don't you get some rest." She gave a small smile as she put her head on his shoulder and just as she was beginning to fall asleep the sound of a squeaking floor board above their heads jolted her awake. The overwhelming actions of the past week came to the forefront of her mind and she began to cry uncontrollably.

Roger put his hand gently over her mouth so her sounds would not be heard and held her tight.

"You've been through an enormous challenge and I can understand how it's affecting you. Please, Christine, please just try to hold on a little bit more. You are so strong and I know you can do it. Please."

His words and her feeling of being so secure in his arms calmed her down and she whispered,"

"I'm okay now and sorry for upsetting you. This is all new to me and I guess my emotions caught up with me.

"Roger, you've been wonderful. I could never have made it this far without you."

He wanted her to stay in his arms forever, this incredible woman. Roger's hands caressed Christine's face and then slowly traveled down her pliant body. He felt her soft breasts and her taut and flat stomach. Christine moaned softly as warmth spread over her. With her hands on his muscular body, he kissed her beautiful mouth.

As their passion quickened it was Roger who found the strength to break away and said,

"Christine, we must wait for the time to be right for us to be together."

Still absorbed in his touch, she had to take a breath, "Okay Roger, you're right, damn it."

The signal came an hour later. The signal that would force Christine to be alone.

CHAPTER FORTY-EIGHT

Joe hoped the car was in good working order, and was relieved that the pill was working.

The car started up and Joe was on his way to the farm country of several miles outside Lille.

The underground contacts, both a farmer and his wife had been alerted to Joe's arrival and they constantly looked through the window and waited. He finally arrived. They could see him driving onto their property and ran outside to meet him.

"Hurry, go inside. Give my wife your uniform and we will put it into the car. I have some of my clothes ready for you to wear. I will then pull the car around the back near the barn. Don't worry we will get rid of the car and the uniform."

"Why?"

"The word is out that there's an imposter posing as SS Officer Eric Meyers."

Joe responds with a rush of anger,

"Damn it. That's bad news."

Once inside the wife gave Joe the clothing and he went into the bedroom and changed.

When he came out the wife said,

"There's also a door to door search for Christine and Roger. We don't know where they are, but I know that the Gestapo is turning every place inside out. It is just a matter of time before they catch them."

"I think I know where they should be. Look, please get me something to eat and some water."

"We can also give you a pair of old boots that will help keep your feet warm."

"I'm going to leave as soon as I take a quick nap. Then I'm going to go where I hope I can find Roger and Christine before the Gestapo. I have a plan and I need to work it though."

Joe was formulating how he would reach Christine and Roger and then be able to maneuver their escape.

"When you're ready my husband will take you in our hay wagon to the outskirts of Lille. His permit does not allow him to go into the city. You will have to walk the rest of the way."

"That's okay and thank you."

After a short nap, he prepared himself to leave and embark on his journey. Dressed in simple attire, the farmer's wife gave him a knapsack with some bread and cheese.

He hoped that since they would be looking for a man in Meyer's SS Officer Uniform he would not send off any alarms and he could blend in with the villagers.

CHAPTER FORTY-NINE

Still together, Rheinhold asks, "Peter, did you ever find out where the real Eric Meyers is?"

"I found out that he was on rest leave in Laon, France, and had our people try and reach him. No luck so far."

"Hmm, you know that he could be dead."

"I know, Hans, and that makes it even more important that we get these monsters."

After coordinating their ideas, they concluded that these three must be collaborating.

Peter's devious mind is swimming with thoughts of how to eliminate Rheinhold from any acclaim.

Peter believed that Rheinhold did not know about the vital briefcase that Emil Brandt had brought home on the day he died.

Peter thought to himself,

"Had Brandt worked out the final formulas? If so, Christine must have the contents and the answers. I have to get hold of those papers.

"Was Emil killed because of the papers in his briefcase and was it her assignment to get those papers at all costs?

"Was her job solely as executioner with Emil Brandt her target?

"Where are the papers now?

"Were they handed over to the British? In which case her role is finished and now she just wants to escape?

"Who is her accomplice? Was his job just to help her escape?"

Suddenly a message of extreme importance was delivered.

Christine and her accomplice were spotted by an informant in the city of Lille.

Peter thought quickly as they both read the message,

"Hans, do you think it would be better for you to work on the Eric Meyer's imposter while I head for Christine?"

Rheinhold had to think, think wisely about what was more important. The woman or the possible killer of Eric Meyers? Had he known about the briefcase and the incredible answers on paper he would have chosen Christine. But he didn't know and so,

"Peter, you go ahead to Lille and I'll try and find out more about the imposter."

Peter agreed, "We'll search all the houses in that town."

Rheinhold nodded agreement and as soon as Peter left, he called in the two SS Officers that had been waiting outside for instructions.

"Here's what I want you to do. Put out an alert to every train station for our SS Officers to check the credentials of any, I mean any, SS Officer on board or nearby. If any of the papers says Eric Meyers, you make an immediate arrest and contact me directly. Do you understand? We are looking for a spy who probably killed SS Officer Eric Meyers."

CHAPTER FIFTY

As darkness descended, Christine entered the small village realizing that the curfew was in effect. Walking through the streets, trying not to appear obvious, her heart was beating rapidly.

A sudden shout of "Halt" brought her to an abrupt stop.

A young uniformed German soldier appeared from nowhere.

They stared at each other until he said in broken French,

"What are you doing out late? Don't you know of the curfew?"

Responding with her own limited French,

"Lost, I got lost. I am visiting my aunt. I'm so sorry."

As she spoke, her scarf slipped off her head and he was taken aback by her loveliness.

He was momentarily out of words.

She smiled sweetly.

"Please forgive me."

He had only one hour before reporting for duty.

"Oh, okay. You come with me for drink?"

Christine smiled her glistening smile and nodded yes.

The café on the corner was open since German soldiers needed time for relaxation. It was also not unusual to see a German soldier and a French lady drinking together. There were many liaisons between them.

Minimal words were spoken, but she knew just how to flirt and make a man feel as though he was important.

The time for the soldier to report for duty, fortunately for Christine, was upon them.

"Can see again?" He said.

"Yes." He took out his notepad and wrote the address of her aunt. She gave him a fictitious address and prayed he would not come looking for her.

"I must go now, I must report. Go quickly to aunt, curfew must be kept."

"Yes, see you soon, I hope."

They parted and she was able to get away from the smiling German soldier.

She was late getting to 32 Franson Street. Roger had arrived much earlier and by now was frantic that she may have been arrested.

When he heard the coded knocks, he could almost hear his heart stop. The contact opened the door, pulled her in and then Roger swept her up in his arms.

"Thank god you're here. Why so late?"

"Believe it or not I ran into a German soldier who actually asked me to have a drink with him. Thank goodness he only had an hour before he had to report for duty."

"Thank goodness, indeed."

Hours later Joe Matthews found himself at the edge of the same town where Roger and Christine were hiding. Joe moved in and out of sheltered areas and now, early in the morning, found himself amongst the townspeople going about their day's normal activities.

The familiar knock allowed the door to open and for the first time Joe came face to face with Christine Spencer. Roger went over to shake his hand and Christine smiled at him and greeted him warmly. He caught his breath as he had a momentary feeling of having seen her before.

However, he did not react, but simply puts out his hand to shake hers and said,

"Well, Miss Spencer, it's an honor to finally meet the lady of the hour."

"It's a pleasure to meet you, Joe."

They all sat down to converse, to eat and most importantly make the final plans for getting to Calais where a boat will be waiting to bring them across the Channel.

After the plans were finalized, Christine asked Joe,

"Joe, can you tell me what happened to Marta Brauer?"

"I killed her."

His abrupt reply momentarily shocked Christine as she reached for a chair and sat down heavily.

"Why was this necessary?"

"Because she was preparing to kill you. When I saw her I knew she was completely out of control and capable of anything. Besides, there was the danger of her bringing down the entire operation."

Christine knew she should not probe further.

"Okay, no more questions, I need to rest for a little while since I've been walking all night."

He went to the back room, sat on the bed and shut his eyes. Before he could drift off he played in his mind how he had taken care of Marta........

.... Marta opened the door and there unexpectedly stood Joe.

He felt her excitement as she grabbed his arm and coaxed him into the room while babbling, almost incoherently,

"I can't believe it. I cannot believe it. Thank god you're here."

"Calm down, please and tell me why."

"It's, it's about Christine. She is crazy. There are things I have to tell you about her.

Something is wrong with her and she is putting everything in jeopardy. Let us go to a safe place and then I'll tell you."

Now he knew his first instincts were correct, Marta was unbalanced.

"We have some time and I think we should just sit and have a drink while you tell me."

"Yes, that's a good idea. I could really use something." After returning with the brandy that Joe had given her a month before, she gulped it down too fast, but the sting of the liquor made her calmer. While Joe took only a sip, Marta drank another glass full as she sat down on the sofa.

"Marta, please tell me exactly what it is that you think Christine is doing to jeopardize our operation."

"I've been watching her and I know she has secrets Joe, lot's of secrets. Joe, she has to be eliminated. She's going to ruin every-thing. You and I have to be together and plan a new operation. Christine must be disposed of."

Upon hearing these words, Joe slid closer to Marta, put his arm around her shoulder and pulled her close to him as if to give her a kiss. With one quick motion, his hands moved against her throat and pressed tightly. She flung her arms wildly as she struggled against his grip. He kept the pressure going until she could no longer resist. He was surprised at how strong she was and how long it took him to subdue her.

Marta was dead.

He signaled his men who were waiting for their orders and they moved quickly to remove the body.....

It will be a long time before Joe could let go of these images.

CHAPTER FIFTY-ONE

Peter Gruder, along with his men, commanded a search of every house in the village. Peter was becoming desperate to find Christine and the briefcase.

Since the town had so many houses, he ordered his men to split up and cover as many as possible.

"I'm going to check some places by myself. I need you to investigate another street."

He would come to 32 Franson Street and not just knock but bang on the door with the butt of his luger. He saw a dim light from the street and knows someone is home.

Without waiting another moment he kicks in the door and is shocked to see Christine and her accomplice standing next to the table.

With his gun now pointed at them he walked over to Christine with his face contorted with rage, and with one arm grabs her arm so tightly she could feel the blood rushing through her veins.

"You bitch, where is the briefcase? I want the briefcase now." Christine, shrinking back from Gruder's grip said (loudly enough for Joe to hear),

"The briefcase? I got rid of that a long time ago."

"You're lying. I'll give you two minutes to give me that briefcase or I'll shoot your friend here first and then you."

Christine, seeing his hatred knows he will follow through with the threat. She stalls just long enough for Joe to climb out the back window and make his way around the front where the door remained open.

Silently, Joe barefooted, crept up behind Gruder and brought the butt of his gun down on his head and watched Gruder fall to the floor unconscious.

Joe closed the door after looking around outside.

Getting the rope, stuffing a cloth over his mouth and tying him to the chair, they sat down to decide what they would do.

There was no way they were going to be able to move quietly to their last town without being captured and so they had to formulate a plan of action.

In the meantime,

Rheinhold waited impatiently at the station for word about his order regarding Eric Meyers. After a couple of hours, there was finally a knock on his door.

"Enter."

Standing in the doorway was Joseph, one of the men who was with Peter Gruder when they discovered the body of Emil.

"Oh, excuse me Sir, I was told Herr Gruder was here."

"He's on assignment. What do you want him for?"

Joseph replied unaware of Peter Gruder's deceit,

"Well Sir, I'm sure you know that we were looking for Emil Brandt's briefcase as soon as we found his body. I was just told we found it in a garbage can on Holson Street in Berlin. Unfortunately, it is empty, but I thought it was important to tell Herr Gruder since he was so anxious to find it."

Rheinhold was burning inside. He held his fury as he surmised to himself, "That son of a bitch. He is after Brant's work for von Braun and he said nothing. No wonder he wanted to get to Christine before I did. That bastard. I'll get him."

Then he did say aloud.

"Oh yes, of course I know and thank you. You can go. Call in Officer Romer."

When Romer appeared, he ordered him to get a vehicle so he could get to Gruder.

Rheinhold would come up against much more than expected.

While Rheinhold was plotting against Gruder, little did he know that Peter was unconscious, tied to a chair and at the mercy of the three agents he was seeking.

CHAPTER FIFTY-TWO

Roger was just through telling Joe that Christine had memorized the data and that the papers had been burned. She had stored the formulas and computations in her extraordinary mind.

Emil Brandt's findings, now embedded in her mind, held the key to von Braun's success. Therefore, she's the person that must be transported across the channel. All British and American agents consider this their highest priority.

In deciding how to get her out of France and back to England, Joe would escort Christine while Roger would follow with Peter Gruder as his hostage. This would also provide a better cover since Joe is obviously much older. Joe thought the best way to insure their escape would be to travel as father and daughter.

Peter Gruder opened his eyes and when Roger saw he was awake said, up against his face,

"Do you want to live?" Of course Gruder shook his head yes.

"Then you will do exactly as I say or I will kill you. Remember we have already killed several of your countrymen and one more won't make a difference."

Peter nods vehemently.

The resistance had prepared for their arrival with a set of forged papers that reflected a German family. The underground contact, still at the house, handed Joe and Christine their papers. Since the last name was the same for both they could now act as father and daughter.

If questioned, they would say they're on the way to see her brother, a German soldier, wounded in a Calais hospital.

They waited until daylight to leave among the other inhabitants of Lille.

After they left Roger looked outside and saw a German vehicle at the end of the block. He went over to Gruder and released the ropes around his legs but left his hands tied tightly. He put Gruder's coat over his hands and with his own gun, now equipped with a silencer, pressed it to Peter's side said,

"We're going to leave now and walk over to the jeep. I warn you to let me do the talking. One word from you and you're dead."

Gruder, with an expression of true hatred, nodded okay.

Outside, just as they were approaching the jeep, a young soldier returning to his jeep came around the corner and immediately walked up to Gruder with his formal salute. He recognized Gruder as a very important man.

"Herr Gruder, is there anything you want me to do?"

Roger replied to his question in German,

"I have a gun at Herr Gruder's side and will shoot him and then you if you don't get into this jeep and obey my orders."

The soldier thought for just one moment and knew that he had to protect Gruder from any harm. He nodded yes and jumped into the jeep as Roger and Peter sat in the back.

As the ride continued with Roger's directions, Peter, knowing that he would be killed, made a last ditch effort to save himself. He shouted to the driver, "Do something. Crash the car."

Hearing these words, Roger released the trigger into Peter's body with the sound disguised by the silencer.

He warned the driver,

"Keep your eyes on the road. If you crash this jeep, Gruder and you are dead."

A frightened young recruit was terrified and did not know what to do.

Now, Roger put the gun up against the back of his neck and ordered him,

"You just drive or you're dead."

The soldier kept driving. The sounds of the jeep on the road hid the sound of Peter Gruder gasping his last breath.

Nearing Calais, Roger instructed the driver to pull into a wooded area at the side of the road. As soon as the jeep came to a halt, Roger shot him in the back of the head. He pushed him to the side, jumped in front and drove deep into the woods.

He would make the rest of the trip on foot.

Their resistance contact in Lille had waited until they all left and then signaled the resistance in Calais to be on the lookout for Christine, Joe and Roger with Peter Gruder as Roger's hostage.

Roger arrived first at their rendezvous and was waiting anxiously for Joe and Christine.

It was a smooth and uneventful walk for Joe and Christine through the village. Now, keeping to the back roads, they continued their trek until they could blend in with the inhabitants of Calais.

The happy reunion with Roger brought a momentary relief of tension.

Now the weather was the most important factor in their escape.

The Channel waters were unpredictable and they were in constant touch with England for the best opportunity to make the crossing.

They had to wait for the right time.

This would give Rheinhold his chance for revenge.

CHAPTER FIFTY-THREE

Herr Rheinhold entered Lille after being told that Peter Gruder was last seen on Franson Street.

Just turning dark, all the residents dare not disobey the curfew.

Rheinhold, assisted by several of his men looked forward to confronting Peter Gruder and rendering out a suitable and excruciating punishment.

He invaded every house and the only one on the street that was empty was 32 Franson Street.

Just a touch and the door opened. Rheinhold gave the order to search every inch of the two rooms.

His men reported they found nothing.

Where was Peter Gruder?

Rheinhold was not a stupid man. He realized that Peter had discovered their impending escape route. Thinking to himself,

"That bastard must be on their tail and once more he's a step ahead of me."

The only possible direction to leave France would be Calais and the English Channel.

Rheinhold is bewildered, enraged and filled with desire for Peter's demise. He must, however, keep his thoughts straight and clear.

He said to himself, "What do I do now? How do I beat him at his own game? I have to do this one step at a time."

Aloud he orders,

"Get my car and a very good driver. I'm in a hurry and must move quickly."

The only place it could be was Calais.

He knew he couldn't search all of Calais, but deployed his men to check the houses closest to the coast and the surrounding area.

He thought the best way to reach the spies would be at the coastline and his objective now had a dual purpose. To find the enemy and then destroy Peter Gruder.

Just outside of Calais, as the dawn broke through in the woods, the body of Peter Gruder was discovered.

Rheinhold wanted to see Gruder chastised, but never dead.

This gave him an excuse to enlist the aid for more troops. After all, this important member of the hierarchy had been brutally killed by enemy agents trying to leave the country with invaluable material.

Another part of Rheinhold was actually experiencing a self-satisfied inkling of how he could win the prestige that would have been Peters.

CHAPTER FIFTY-FOUR

England informed Joe that there was an upcoming break in the weather and they had to act immediately.

The Trawler, sitting in readiness, was signaled to begin the crossing to France.

The window for a favorable opening for the crossing was very brief.

They must be ready and waiting at the coastline to embark within minutes.

Rheinhold, focusing his binoculars on the coastline spotted all three operatives together.

This was going to be Rheinhold's glorious hour. He quickly sent a runner to gather his men together. Rheinhold would arrest or, if necessary, shoot.

Those three must never be allowed to escape.

Joe, with his binoculars, focused on the boat in the distance.

"Christine, Roger, I see it coming. Everyone ready? We only have a couple of minutes to get on the boat since I can see the currents are changing."

Watching the impending arrival of the boat, they suddenly hear the sound of men behind them.

Now the boat comes in as far as it can to avoid the rocks.

"Hope you can swim because that's what we have to do, now, right now."

Joe, Christine and Roger plunged into the water and swam toward the boat.

Rheinhold shouts to his men. "Kill them, they must not get away."

Joe, a very strong swimmer is the first to reach the vessel. The men, hanging over the side, threw a rope and Joe grabbed on to it and with his easy agility quickly climbed aboard.

Christine, following right behind needed more help. She grabbed on to the rope as Joe leaned over to catch her with Roger assisting her from below. As Christine is pulled onto the boat, Roger, their friend and colleague, was shot in the head and fell back into the water.

Christine screams, "Get him, and help him."

The Captain says, "He's gone and we must leave instantly."

With that, the boat pulls away into the dark at great speed.

Christine begins to sob with grief, "Oh this wonderful man; I will miss him. He was my partner and savior and now he's gone."

Joe put his arms around her and tried to comfort her. "I know this is a terrible loss for you and all of us. He was a devoted servant of the crown and will be sadly missed."

Rheinhold, in the meantime, stood at the shore, stamping his feet in frustration and anger. Yelled to his men, "You let them get away. How could you not have shot all of them? You inept idiots."

It's all over and Rheinhold knows it.

CHAPTER FIFTY-FIVE

At the shore in Dover England, their arrival is met with great relief, adoration and much sorrow for the loss of one of their most important agents.

They had to take Joe to the hospital after he admits that he was in severe pain with an ulcer.

Christine was taken to a hotel for much needed sleep before her debriefing. She had wanted to go with Joe to the hospital, but they told her he needed to be examined and then to rest.

She felt so alone and sad. Roger, her loyal partner, was gone and she missed him terribly.

England, knowing that they had temporarily averted disaster, waited impatiently to extract Christine's knowledge. They had to control their excitement and let her rest.

She was ready to be questioned after eight hours of deep sleep.

The probing would require many hours of questions and answers. They were awed by her remarkable retention for detail of Emil Brandt's brilliant conclusions.

A senior representative of the United States Government, listening to her espouse the formulas thought to himself,

"This is someone we really need in this time of crisis."

Later when the representative met with Joe Matthews, who was now feeling better after receiving the proper medication, commended him on a job well done. He asked,

"You must know we want you to continue working with the War Department."

"But what about my illness? I thought that would end my career in the field."

"Listen, with the right diet and medication that should not be a problem. You are too valuable to lose.

We also, at the same time, hope you will be able to convince Christine to continue as well."

"Let me think it over." He knew he would say yes to any assignment. After all, he wanted to be part of the war effort.

After the tedious interrogation, an exhausted Christine still wanted to see Joe.

They agreed and took her to the hospital where Joe was resting on his bed. Framed in the doorway Joe looked up and his heart lurched. He thought, "What is it about her that's making me feel as though I know her?"

As she approached, he shook his head to clear his thoughts and greeted her warmly.

"Well, I hear you're feeling better."

Joe replied,

"Yes I am much better. If you're up to it I'd like to talk to you about something."

"Sure."

"I've been approached by the United States high command to continue my work."

"Joe, that's wonderful."

"Christine, they have also indicated that they want you as well."

"What?"

"Yeah, I guess they think we make a formidable team."

Christine had been forced to become a spy but now, after being able to succeed at something so paramount in today's world crisis, she actually felt excited about the offer. However, she had to think about her mother.

"Joe, I miss my mother. We are very close. I need to go home and see her."

Joe said,

"I think they'll probably fly your mother to Washington to see you and spend some time."

"Really? All the way from Chicago?"

Again, Joe felt the same jolt.

"I think they will. Chicago? I knew someone from Chicago. What area do you come from?"

"Hyde Park."

"Oh my, were you born in Chicago?"

"Yes, all my life. Who did you know?" She asked,

"A woman I once met in a movie theater that I adored."

"That's really something. My mother once told me she had fallen in love with a man she only knew for four days and she met him in a movie theater. He promised to write to her, but never did. I really do not think she ever got over it.

"Tell me Joe, what was your lady's name?"

"Lee."

"Lee? Wow, that's too much."

"Why?"

"That's what they call my mother, its short for Elizabeth."

Joe held his breath, but he had to ask,

"Tell me, because you never know, what was your mother's maiden name?

"Bachman."

Joe could not believe what he was hearing. Again, he felt compelled to ask,

"In reading the dossier on you, I forget your birthday."

"October 20, 1918."

His mind was whirling back to Lee, his love, his Lee. He never forgot the date when they made love. On that cold day in January 1918.

Holding in this remarkable awareness, he smiled at Christine. The kind of smile a father gives a daughter.

THE END

Made in the USA
Middletown, DE
09 September 2019